THE LONESOME COWBOY'S ABDUCTED BRIDE

MONTANA WESTWARD BRIDES BOOK THREE

AMELIA ROSE

CONTENTS

This book is dedicated to all of my faithful readers, without whom I would be nothing. I thank you for the support, reviews, love, and friendship you have shown me as we have gone through this journey together. I am truly blessed to have such a wonderful readership.

CHAPTER 1

$\mathcal{T}$he late summer air ruffled Eddie's hair as he sat astride his horse in the back pastures. He was watching over the herd as they roamed and grazed, mindful of any predators that might be lurking from a distance. With the wide-open spaces of Montana stretching as far as the eye could see, it was easy to spot people coming and going, but more importantly, if a coyote or mountain lion was wandering about.

Eddie smiled to himself as he ran his hand through is light brown hair. It had been almost a year and a half since he'd come to work for Dr. Slater on his cattle ranch. For the first time in his life, he was finally feeling his feet on solid ground. He had a stable income for once, a place to rest his head at night, and three home-cooked meals he could look forward to each day. His bosses were considerate men. Where Dr. Slater had a great sense of humor, his foreman, Gray, was very straight to the point. Although, he often proved that he had a solid funny bone in him.

Together with his brother, Sawyer, they lived on the ranch in the bunkhouse, learning the way of the cowboy. Much had happened in their short time on the cattle ranch. The eldest ranch hand, Jensen, had passed away during a brutal winter. He was an old-timer who had done his job well for many years. But the Montana winters were always daunting. Cold winds, piles of snow, and days where you couldn't leave the house because of the freezing temperatures. This past winter had been no exception and had unfortunately taken a toll on Jensen. When he did pass away, it had taken days before they were able to dig a proper grave and hold a small service for the feisty man.

The Slater Ranch had lost a great soul, but it had also gained two little ones. Lucy Slater had given birth to a redheaded little girl that looked just like Lucy. They'd named her Francene after Dr. Slater's mother. Eddie couldn't help but laugh over how doting Francene's parents were. Dr. Slater had become a very worrisome parent while Lucy let the little girl toddle all about the house. The love between Dr. Slater and his wife had only grown stronger, and Eddie wouldn't be surprised if Lucy would be expecting again soon.

In addition to the bunch was Gray and Martha's son, Samuel, which had been a hilarious announcement since Dr. Slater thought Gray had named his son after him. But in fact, it was to honor Martha's father. However, Dr. Sam Slater still teased Gray about it endlessly. Together, Lucy and Martha enjoyed raising their little ones together, as well as managing their women's boutique in town. Now, Eddie couldn't help but shake his head at that. He always thought that women were better off at home, raising children and taking care of the cooking for the family. It was different to see two women working, minding the children, and taking care of a household. Though, Gray had gone back to helping with the cooking; before Lucy had come along, he'd been the ranch's cook and had reclaimed that title again with the women working in town.

Eddie sighed as a strong summer breeze swept over the open pasture. It was quite early in the morning and already the day felt hot. He let his hand fall from the reins to his saddle bag at his side as he double-checked the amount of water he had in his canteen. Then, he pulled out a date and handed it to the furry fellow on this shoulder.

"Looks like it's going to be another hot day, Jack. We should probably go post up in the shade," Eddie said to the brown capuchin monkey that sat on his shoulder, where he resided most of the day. The monkey simply chattered in return as he ate the date. Eddie made his way slowly through the herd, guiding his gelding through the cattle to a shady tree in the distance. The moment Eddie had guided his horse underneath the long branches, Jack climbed off his shoulder and up into the tree before Eddie could dismount.

"Hey, don't get stuck up in the tree again, Jack. The last time that happened you didn't come down for three days and got stuck in a rainstorm. Looked like a drowned rat to me," Eddie called up into the tree. Jack simply bared his teeth at Eddie, something Eddie considered to be some sort of smile. There was much about Jack he was still trying to learn, but he enjoyed having the monkey around simply to see what he would do next.

As Eddie settled back against the trunk of the tree, his eyes switching between the moving cattle and Jack above him, he recalled the night he'd gotten Jack. It had been a wild night at Handy's. He and Sawyer were up to their usual antics of trying to impress the ladies. But he'd settled down at a poker table when he realized that there was a traveler trying his luck at the game. The thing that amused Eddie the most that this British man had a monkey on his shoulder. Wanting to learn what the monkey was all about, Eddie had taken a seat at the table, much to the chagrin of the other players. Eddie was known for his poker skills, but he wasn't interested in money that night. He'd never seen a monkey before and wanted to know the traveling man's story.

As Eddie had begun playing round after round, trying not to draw to much attention to himself by winning every hand like normal, Eddie had learned from the British man that he'd bartered for the monkey from a group of Chinamen. At the time, the fellow had wanted to take the monkey back home to England with him. But the more Eddie watched the monkey sitting ever so obediently on his master's shoulder, the more Eddie had wanted the furry animal himself. Eddie had then started to play the game seriously, intent on pressuring the British fellow to give up the monkey. He'd played the man all night, and finally had left with the monkey in hand.

"What in the world do you plan to do with a monkey? You can't even eat it if you change your mind," Sawyer had said when he'd shown his brother the furry thing.

"I'm going to train it just like a cattle dog. He'll help me keep an eye over the cattle," Eddie had said with a wide grin. He'd learned all he could from the British man about raising Jack successfully, but the man had been so angry about losing his pet that Eddie hadn't learned very much. Therefore, there had been a major learning curve for Eddie.

Furthermore, Dr. Slater and Gray weren't too happy with Eddie bringing a monkey back to the ranch. Eddie quickly learned to keep Jack on a leash after the monkey had gone on a tangent and ripped Lucy's curtains. Lucy had to admit that Jack was cute, but it was no longer allowed in the house. Gray had been worried that Jack would spook the cattle instead of keeping them in line, and it had taken a lot of convincing to the foremen to allow Eddie to keep Jack in the bunkhouse. But even though Jack was very cute and could do a few amusing tricks, he had a wild side to him that often got on everyone's nerves.

But to Eddie, Jack had been the friend he'd been looking for. Though he loved his brother Sawyer, Eddie felt like they were headed in two different directions. Eddie longed to settle and put down roots, while Sawyer was always ready for the next adventure. Though Sawyer was a silent fellow, he loved the thrills of life. That's why together as brothers they were often asked to be assistant deputies for Sheriff Josh Ryder because they worked well together and often loved a good chase. They were great shots under pressure and often worked great together, even though they bickered here and there. Sawyer loved the adrenaline of chasing down bad guys, but Eddie had come to realize that there was more in life than a good thrill.

As Eddie sat looking over the herd, trying to keep an eye

on Jack at the same time, he started to think about what he wanted most in life. Though he loved having Jack and got to work closely with his brother, he knew there was more to life than that. After coming to stay on the ranch, he'd gotten to see firsthand what married life was like. Lucy and Dr. Slater were a great match, even though Lucy had been a mail-order-bride. They'd created a wonderful life together and obviously loved each other.

The same could be said for Martha and Gray. Even though there was a large age gap between the two, they still loved each other dearly. So much so, that even though Samuel technically had a different father, Gray still loved and raised him as his own.

After watching the two couples closely for the last year and a half, Eddie started to think that perhaps now was the time to start thinking about finding a wife of his own. He knew that it would be difficult since he knew most of the women in the area more personally than he should. And after seeing how successful both Dr. Slater and Gray had been after finding mail-order-brides, Eddie started to consider doing the very same thing.

It was a thought that often came to him during the hot hours when he needed something to keep his mind busy, or he would focus too much on the heat. He continued to go back and forth over the idea since he didn't know if he was the type of person that would interest a lady. Though he had an established position at the ranch that paid well enough, he didn't have his own home. And to make matters more interesting, he had a pet monkey that often caused more trouble than good. He wasn't very confident in the idea of finding a match, and therefore had put off physically placing an ad for some time.

"There you are!" called Sawyer away in the distance. He rode over to where Eddie was resting in the shade. As his brother approached, he stood and shielded his eyes from the sun to get a better look at his brother. Where Eddie was tall and lengthy, Sawyer was shorter with broad shoulders. But they both had light brown hair and blue eyes.

As Sawyer guided his horse underneath the tall branches to reach the shade, Jack jumped down to a nearby branch, startling Sawyer.

"I swear, one of these days I'm going to shoot that damn monkey," Sawyer said as he tried to shoo Jack away with his cowboy hat. Jack simply bared his teeth and screeched with laughter.

"Come on. You can't deny that you love Jack just as much as I do," Eddie reasoned.

"That's only when Jack is teasing someone else," Sawyer said. "Speaking of, Mrs. Lucy says lunch is ready. I'll take your spot for a bit."

"Much appreciated," Eddie said as he pulled himself back up into the saddle of his gelding and clicked his tongue three times to tell Jack it was time to go. But Jack remained where he was in the tree, looking down at Eddie with pleading eyes.

"Looks like the fellow wants to stay with his uncle," Eddie said with a smirk as he turned his eyes to Sawyer. He watched as Sawyer rolled his eyes before shrugging his shoulders.

"Never thought I'd be a monkey's uncle," Sawyer said as he dismounted. Eddie couldn't resist laughing as he clicked his heels against the gelding, sending the horse into a canter.

As Eddie traveled across the pasture to the ranch house, Eddie thought that things were a lot different than either one of them could have ever imagined. They had steady employment, a roof over their heads, and were saving their money instead of spending it all every weekend at Handy's. At least, Eddie knew that he was saving most of his pay now and hoped that his brother was doing the same. Eventually, Eddie wanted space of his own. And perhaps one day he'd finally meet a woman he'd want to settle down with.

As Eddie made his way towards the ranch house, he kept contemplating if now was the time to write that ad.

CHAPTER 2

*F*iona Wilkins found refuge from the Boston heat by lounging in the drawing room. It was much cooler in that part of the house as it was positioned on the opposite side from where the sun was. The room had been positioned precisely in this manner for her mother, Mrs. Melisa Wilkins, so she could entertain guests during the warmer months. But since her mother was out visiting friends, that meant that Fiona could find peace and quiet in the cooler room until her parents made her do something else.

Fiona sighed with boredom as she set aside the novel she had been trying to read. It no longer interested her since she'd read it three times. Her parents often didn't let her purchase novels because they were afraid the books would tarnish her mind. But it was one of the few pleasures in life that Fiona treasured. She had a small collection of western novels that she could lose herself in. Though she hid them underneath her bed, she considered them one of her prized possessions. But since her parents didn't often let her shop alone and were always very watchful of Fiona and her decisions, she hadn't been able to purchase a new novel in months.

"Good afternoon, Miss Fiona. Here's some lemonade and cucumber sandwiches I put together for you," Mrs. Dickens said as she came into the drawing room wheeling a tea cart towards her.

"How lovely, Mrs. Dickens. Thank you so much for thinking of me," Fiona said, brightening up. The housekeeper had always been very mindful of Fiona's needs and Fiona considered the older woman one of her closer friends. Fiona's earliest memories had been of Mrs. Dickens and she didn't know how else she had managed to survive without the woman since her parents were more concerned about their social appearance than their daughter.

"Of course, darling. The last thing I want is you getting overheated on this hot day. I'd invite you to join me in the kitchen today if it wasn't so warm. It seems your parents are gone for the afternoon and I could teach you how to make those croissants you always love, but it's just too hot today," Mrs. Dickens said, rambling on like normal.

Fiona simply smiled in return as she took a long drink of her lemonade before taking a bite of the cucumber sandwich. Fiona hummed with pleasure as she ate. "These are delicious, Mrs. Dickens. Did you use the cucumbers from the garden?" Fiona asked.

"Indeed, Miss Fiona. I know your mother wasn't keen on you having a garden, but I think it's done you some good to have something to do outside," Mrs. Dickens said with a chuckle. Fiona couldn't help but join her.

"My goodness, the look on Mother's face when I told her I wanted to learn how to garden. That was precious, for sure," Fiona replied as they laughed together about it.

"I know you'll marry well-off, Miss Fiona, but I'm so proud of you for pursuing the things that interest you the most," Mrs. Dickens said, as she took a hold of the tea cart and began wheeling it out of the drawing room. "You just call if you need anything."

As Mrs. Dickens left the drawing room, Fiona let out a sigh and leaned back against the settee, tucking her feet under her in a very unladylike fashion. If her mother had spotted her doing such a thing, then she would surely be scolded for the behavior. But when her parents were not around, Fiona did her best to do as she pleased.

Though she did love her parents dearly, sometimes she thought of them as very overbearing. And since she'd turned eighteen-years-old, they'd been pressuring her even more. Where Mrs. Wilkins was constantly bickering with Fiona about how she acted and dressed, Mr. Wilkins was constantly hosting dinner parties with every prestigious family in the area that had an eligible son to showcase to Fiona. Every gentleman Fiona had been introduced to since her eighteenth birthday had been more boring than the next. None of them had offered Fiona even a morsel of interest as they all planned to follow after their fathers in the world of business.

Even though Fiona did enjoy all the finer things in life, she was deadly bored of socialite life. She didn't care about balls or dinner parties, the latest fashions, or gossiping with other ladies her age. Instead, she longed for the adventurous life of the heroines she read about in her novels. She dreamed of traveling out West and seeing how people really lived and survived each day. The untamed West called to her both night and day- it was what had inspired her to start gardening. It was a crucial skill that all the heroines had to learn to do, and she thought she might try her hand at it. Now she had a bountiful garden full of all sorts of vegetables that Mrs. Dickens had been using in her cooking. Fiona had even learned how to make a few dishes when her parents didn't know about it.

Fiona knew that her Western dreams were simply just that. She had many fantasies that she knew would never come true. The likelihood of her father allowing her to travel out West was a non-existent one. Just suggesting that they take a trip as a family would probably cause her mother to faint from shock. She knew her mother despised anything that was dirty or difficult. She was born a socialite and would always enjoy this type of lifestyle. But Fiona craved something more than city gossip and fancy clothes. She wanted a life that was more meaningful than getting married, living in luxury, and having babies.

Fiona tucked back a strand of her honey colored hair as she leaned her head back on a plush pillow. She closed her blue eyes as she stretched out her legs before her. Her mind floated to what she pictured to be wide-open plains, a light breeze blowing around her as she looked as far as she could see of the countryside. She could listen to birds chirping all day long as the city faded away from her mind. She was standing in her garden and watching the horizon as she waited for her cowboy to come home from the fields, having watched over their cattle all day. She would then make something delicious for herself and her husband for dinner, and then they would...

Fiona was pulled from her daydream as the drawing room door was pulled open and the butler, Mr. Bentley, came walking quickly into the room. Fiona opened her eyes and sat up just as he said, "Miss Chantelle is here to see you," before the young lady herself came floating into the room as though she owned the place. Fiona quickly stood and smoothed down her blue silk dress, hoping she didn't look to disheveled from lounging about all day.

"Oh, Fiona, darling. You must be beside yourself with grief," Chantelle said as she came into the room, sashaying her hips in a dramatic way as she handed Fiona a newspaper. Fiona smiled at Mr. Bentley and dipped her head, dismissing him as he swiftly left the room, sliding the door shut.

"I simply do not know what you speak of," Fiona said in a calm voice as she sat once more. Chantelle took a seat close to her as she smoothed down her muslin dress. Fiona would agree that muslin would have been more comfortable on a hot day like today, but her mother insisted she wear silk, in case she had a visitor. At this moment, Fiona thought her mother had been correct in that demand.

"Look at the engagement announcements, darling. You will surely be shocked to read who Miss Genève has been engaged to," Chantelle said in a very dramatic voice. Though the lady was two years younger than Fiona, she liked to act well beyond her age. Since their mothers were close friends, Chantelle took it upon herself to visit with Fiona, and often without a previous announcement or invitation. And since Fiona was quite used to these types of visits, she simply did her best to please her guest and bide her time before she could find a way to escape.

So, Fiona opened the newspaper and made her way to the announcements until she found Genève's name. "It seems that Mr. Prescott has offered his hand in marriage to Miss Genève. That sounds pleasant enough for her," Fiona said, as she folded the paper once more and looked up at Chantelle.

"You must be filled with such anger to learn that Mr. Prescott overlooked you and instead made his offer to that lowly Genève," Chantelle said with such passion that Fiona was certain that the woman had rehearsed this speech many times before visiting her. Fiona instead remained calmed and refrained from rolling her eyes.

"No, Chantelle. I am not moved at all by the announcement. I had no attachment to Mr. Prescott, and I can't think to reason why you would think I would," Fiona said, as she set the newspaper aside and served Chantelle a glass of lemonade. At least it gave her a moment of silence as they both took a long drink.

"Why, it's all your mother has spoken of all morning. She explained how close you two had become and that she thought he would propose to you rather soon," Chantelle explained. Now Fiona was angry as she learned the source of the rumor. She wanted to throttle her own mother for being so flighty.

"Well, my dear, you've heard it from the horse's mouth. I had no attachment to Mr. Prescott and can be truly happy for Genève," Fiona said, as she handed Chantelle a plate with a few cucumber sandwiches on it.

"No thank you, darling. I'm trying to watch my figure. I shall be attending the ball this Saturday and don't want to eat anything that I might regret later," Chantelle said as she refused the plate. Fiona simply set it back on the tea cart and tried to keep her composure. She had forgotten about the ball and now dreaded it even more than when she'd first heard of its existence. She feared what type of gown her mother had chosen for her to wear, and the men her father would force her to meet.

"What do you plan to wear to the ball?" Fiona asked, knowing the question would occupy Chantelle for some time and remove them from their current topic of discussion. The question worked like a charm, and for the next half hour the ladies talked about Chantelle's dress and the gentlemen she hoped to entice.

"That all sounds quite lovely, my dear. But you must excuse me. This heat has done dreadful things to my nerves and I must go lay down now so I can have my strength for this Saturday. But I do appreciate you stopping by to look after me and to bring me a paper," Fiona said in her most kindly voice, as she stood, paper in hand, using it to cover up the novel she'd been reading earlier.

"Of course, darling. I should probably do the same. What a fantastic idea," Chantelle said as she stood. "Do tell your mother I stopped by." And with that, Chantelle sashayed out of the room like a queen.

Once Chantelle left the house, Fiona let out a long sigh as she left the drawing room and took the stairs up to her room. It would be warmer in her room, but at least she wouldn't be disturbed. The house was rather large with multiple rooms that were often left vacant. The house had been designed for guests and events, but besides the routine dinner party, the house saw little life. It was a dull thing to Fiona who saw the house as wasted space. But once she made it to her room and locked the door behind her, she found that this was the safest place in the whole world.

She tucked her novel safely underneath her bed and set the paper on her writing desk before stripping out of her silk gown. She felt much more comfortable in her simple under garments, and in the privacy of her own room with the door locked, she felt comfortable enough to wear what she wanted.

"Women of the West only wear chamise and day gowns," Fiona mumbled to herself as she put the silk gown away in her wardrobe of silk gowns. The sight almost disgusted her knowing the cost of it all. The amount alone would pay for her ticket out West. Letting out another sigh, Fiona sat down at her writing desk and started to flip through the paper. She was hoping to find something of interest when she stumbled across the matrimonial section.

Though she did intend to marry one day, she hadn't really put much thought into it since her father was always pressing her to meet one gentleman or another. The thought of marrying hadn't been something to cause her dread most of the time, but as she saw the recent wedding announcements, she wondered how many of these matches were made out of love. If Fiona was ever going to marry, she was certain she'd only say, "I do," if it was to someone she really loved. There hadn't been a man yet that had made her think she could possibly love someone one day. She wondered if she would ever meet someone that could capture her heart like the heroines in her novels.

As Fiona read through the paper, her eyes were caught on a particular set of bold letters: "Mail-Order-Brides Wanted for Cowboys," the heading read. Fiona's heart did a flip as she started to read over the announcement. It was an advert explaining how an agency was looking to match young ladies to cowboys out West who needed a wife. And with the West having a limited number of women, it wasn't unusual to see these types of ads. But there was something about this one that interested Fiona. She'd always wanted to meet a real cowboy, and she knew she wouldn't marry a gentleman of Boston. Then perhaps she could meet someone out West and truly have a reason to go?

A smile came to Fiona's lips as she withdrew a piece of writing paper and began to respond to the ad. She'd have to bribe Mr. Bentley to post it for her without her parents ever finding out. It wasn't very hard to do since the older man had a soft spot for a heart. She hadn't been this excited since her last novel arrived in the mail unnoticed. As she wrote her letter to the advertisement, she listed everything that she wanted in a husband and explained that she'd be willing to travel West to meet her husband-to-be.

After Fiona had written her letter and sealed it up, she looked at it for a long time. With this letter, she could be changing her entire future. She couldn't possibly be put into correspondence with a real cowboy that she could possibly fall in love with one day, could she? But even if she did agree to go and meet him, would her father ever let her? Would she need to run away from home to seek a better future for herself? As Fiona sat and thought about what she'd honestly be able to do in leaving Boston behind, she started to reason with herself. But in the end of a long mental debate, Fiona knew she had to do something in order to avoid living a very long dull life.

CHAPTER 3

*E*ddie felt nervous as he sat at the dining table of Dr. Slater's home. The other ranch hands had moved on for the night after dinner had come to an end. He'd told Sawyer to go on without him, asking him to make sure Jack got fed and hadn't destroyed the bunkhouse while they'd come into the ranch house for dinner. Sawyer had given him a puzzled look, but hadn't asked any questions. Now, Eddie sat at the table with Dr. Slater since Lucy had gone to put Francene to bed.

"Something tells me you want to talk about something," Dr. Slater said, after an uncomfortable moment of silence.

"Yeah, there is," Eddie said as he let go of the deep breath he'd been holding in his chest. "I wanted to talk to you about placing an ad in the East for a mail-order-bride."

Dr. Slater looked at him with wide eyes as he seemed to consider what he'd just said. Then, a small smile started to creep onto his face. Eddie couldn't help but smile as well. He felt silly for talking to his boss about such a thing, but there were only two men that he knew of that had mail-order-brides. And since Gray wasn't the personal feelings type of guy, he'd picked the good doctor to talk to. That, and he was certain that Dr. Slater would keep his secret until he was ready to share it with the others.

"Well, Eddie, I'd sure love to help you. When I first met you and your brother, I thought you two were both a pair of hellions that would never be tamed. But I've seen you truly transform this last year, and I think marriage would suit you well. Though, I don't know how many young ladies would love the idea of sharing a home with a monkey," Dr. Slater said, causing them both to laugh heartily.

Eddie nodded his head as his mirth subsided. "Yeah, I reckon there are a few things about me that most young ladies would turn up their noses to. But I don't want to date anyone from our little town. I'm hoping to meet someone from out of state, if possible," Eddie explained.

"Something tells me you're in the same situation as Gray was," Dr. Slater said with a wink. Eddie could only nod his head since he knew that both he and Gray, along with Sawyer, had been womanizers for a long time.

"That would be true, Doc," Eddie replied. He wasn't ashamed of how he'd lived his life. But he also knew that he didn't want to be Gray's age when he decided to consider a wife and kids.

"Well, how about we write something up tonight, and if you like it, I'll take it in to town with me and post it with Mr.

Frost? Ever since Mayor Stavros was able to commission a telegram line to Frost's, he's been biting at the bit to send telegrams as often as he can," Dr. Slater said.

Eddie thought about the offer for a moment. Originally, he'd only intended to talk to Dr. Slater about the idea. The fact that his boss was offering to help him write the ad made him feel a little nervous. But he knew that this would probably be his only way to meet a potential wife, unless the good Lord placed a woman in his path somehow.

"Sure, let's do it," Eddie decided with a smirk.

"That's the spirit. Let me go get us some writing paper," Dr. Slater said as he quickly rose from the table. In the meantime, Eddie tried to think about what his ad would say. What did he want most in a wife? Should he really be all that picky? And what should he say about himself in order to inspire someone to reply to him? By the time Dr. Slater returned to the table with writing paper in hand, along with a quail and ink, Eddie had some sort of idea of what he wanted the ad to say.

"Now, the key to these things is being honest and genuine," Dr. Slater said as he began to write. "You're a hard-working young man with a stable income and fairly good looks."

"Why thank you, Doc. You're not too bad looking yourself," Eddie replied with a chuckle.

"I'm serious, Eddie. The ladies are going to want to know what you look like and what type of guy you are like," Dr. Slater tried to say in a serious tone, though a grin crept at the corner of his mouth.

"Well, I'm a cowboy with a monkey. Make sure that's in there, too. Don't want anyone being surprised if they come out to meet me," Eddie said. He knew that having Jack could be a deal-breaker for most women, but he hoped that there would be someone out there who would love him despite how ornery Jack could be sometime.

"Yes, I think that would be wise. And it will definitely set you apart from all of the others," Dr. Slater agreed as he finished writing the ad. "Alright then, let me know what you think."

As Eddie took the paper. He looked over the words, feeling embarrassed for what he was about to say. "Forgive me, Dr. Slater, but could you read it to me? I was never really good in school," Eddie said sheepishly.

Dr. Slater took back the ad and looked at Eddie for a good moment or two. "Eddie, you can read and write, can't you?" he asked.

Eddie took a deep breath and let it out before replying, "Just a little. Pa took us boys out of school to run the farm when he and Ma both got sick from the flu. They died soon after, and Sawyer and I have been working to survive ever since. There wasn't much time for learning after that," Eddie explained. He knew that he could have taken the opportunity to learn to read and write instead of chasing after women. But he hadn't thought it very important until now.

"Well, I'll read this for you, Eddie, but it's the last time. From now on, in the evenings you're going to have to learn to read and write if you're going to get yourself a mail-order-bride," Dr. Slater said in a firm voice.

"Yes, sir," Eddie replied, knowing there was no point in arguing with the doctor. With that agreement, Dr. Slater read him the ad. Afterwards, Eddie agreed to it, knowing that it was very accurate.

"Well, wish me luck," Eddie said in parting, as he left the ranch house and headed for the bunk house. The night was dark and cool, a refreshing feeling. And as Eddie glanced up at the stars above, he prayed that he'd meet his future wife one day soon.

"BORING. Boring. Dull. Not likely to happen," Fiona mumbled to herself as she looked through the ads the agency had sent her after they'd received her inquiry. So far, she'd been able to hide her correspondence from her parents after offering to pay Mr. Bentley five extra dollars a week to ensure her mail was delivered to her room instead of left on the mantel in the hallway for when her father returned from his office every afternoon. And now she read through her second batch of mail-order-bride ads without much luck.

So far, she'd read several ads about cowboys wanting a woman to cook, clean, raise children, and keep his bed warm at night. They all sounded rather odious and didn't really pique her interest because she was looking for adventure. She didn't want to be someone's live-in servant. Fiona wanted a chance at a real life, and someone to truly love.

Fiona almost took the ads and prepared to rip them up into tiny little pieces so she could dispose of them later without having her parents happen upon and read them, when the last ad caught her attention. The title read, "Cowboy With A Monkey."

"What in the world?" Fiona said as she flattened out the ad and began to read.

'Montana cowboy is seeking a bride from the East. He's a hardworking man with stable employment and a great sense of humor. Has light brown hair and blue eyes that dazzle. But the best part is that Eddie has a pet monkey that can do all sorts of fun tricks. This unique cowboy won't be single for long, so send your letters right away.'

Fiona was giggling by the time she finished reading the ad. She could hardly imagine a cowboy with a pet monkey that could do tricks. She had to admit that this Eddie character was more amusing than any other ad she had read, and probably more charismatic than any gentleman she'd ever been introduced to. As she sat there, she started to bite her lower lip as she tried to decide what to do. She could certainly tear up this ad with the others. But would there ever be a more interesting ad? Knowing that most of them had been rather dull, Fiona decided to save this ad. And as she started to tear up the others, she grew excited about the idea of writing to Eddie right away.

"Who'd you get the letter from, little brother?" Sawyer asked, as they walked towards the barn after having lunch up at the ranch house. Lucy had just come home from her morning shift at the boutique with Francene, bringing home the mail with her. And though Lucy had been kind enough not to pester Eddie about the origins of the letter, since everyone knew how nosy Lucy could be, it seemed that his older brother wouldn't give him the same treatment.

"I have to open it first," Eddie responded as he pocketed the letter. Though he was curious himself to know who the author of the letter was, he hadn't told anyone besides Dr. Slater that he'd placed an ad for a mail-order-bride. He didn't want to share the news with anyone until it was certain that he'd met someone worth sending for. Until then, he wasn't going to give up hope, or allow anyone to stir up his emotions, either.

"Well, aren't you going to open it now?" Sawyer asked as they mounted their horses. But all Eddie did was whistle for Jack, causing the monkey to come running to him from up in the rafters of the barn. The monkey swung down with his tail and landed on Eddie's shoulder. Then with a click of his heels, he sent his gelding to a canter towards the open gate. Not wanting to respond to his brother's question, he made quick work of separating himself from the other man, wanting to seek a moment alone in order to read the letter in private.

As he worked on the far side of the field, keeping an eye on the cattle and making sure the herd was together, he finally took the time to pull the letter from his back pocket. But like Jack often did, he jumped down on the saddle, thinking Eddie had pulled some food from his pocket, and quickly took the letter from Eddie's hand and jumped down to the ground with it.

"Jack, no! Bad monkey! Bring me back that letter," Eddie called as he turned his horse around. As Jack scurried across the ground, dodging between the feet of the cattle and disappearing into the herd, Eddie did his best to follow the monkey, trying not to scatter or disturb the cows. Eventually, Eddie had to dismount and follow the monkey on foot.

"Jack! Jack, get back here!" Eddie called out between whistles he used to summon the furry animal. But nothing seemed to work until he came to the shady tree he often sat under on hot days. It was also the same tree that Jack often seemed to get stuck in. And it was here that Eddie found the monkey high in the trees, eating the corner of the letter.

"Damn monkey!" Eddie cried out as he kicked the tree as hard as he could. The tree shook, scaring Jack to the point where he dropped the letter and clung to the tree. But Eddie was also hollering in pain from where he'd stubbed his toe. By the time the pain had subsided, the letter had finally drifted down to him from the tree above, where Jack remained, clutching one of the top branches.

"That's what you get for stealing from me, Jack! You can stay up there for days for all I care," Eddie called up to the tree. Eddie picked up the letter from the ground then and inspected it, seeing small tears in the envelope and an entire corner wet from where Jack had tried to eat it. Muttering to himself, Eddie pocketed the letter once more and walked away from the tree, needing to find his horse and regroup the herd from where he had scattered it earlier.

Once things seemed to be calm again, Eddie looked around him to be certain he was alone before extracting the letter again, and finally opening it. Inside were three sheets of writing paper, both front and back. He was surprised by the length of the letter, and as he looked down at the fancy cursive letters, Eddie groaned with frustration. He'd been so excited to read the letter, having been practicing every night with Dr. Slater, that he hadn't thought of having to deal with cursive. But as he pressed the letter to his face, hoping to see better, he only groaned louder with frustration.

"Damn it!" Eddie hollered as he folded the letter carefully and placed it back inside the envelope. Now he'd have to wait even longer to discover the contents of the letter.

"I'M SORRY, Eddie. I think Sam got stuck in town with a patient. But if ye want, I can help ya if ye need it," Lucy said as she rocked Francene to sleep in the rocker that Dr. Slater had commissioned Zachariah Welliver, the local furniture maker, to create for Lucy. Eddie had come into the sitting room after dinner had been cleaned up, hoping to figure out when the doctor would be home so he could help Eddie read the letter with him. And now he was faced with an even harder decision. Tell Lucy why he needed help reading the letter and who the letter was from, or, have to wait until tomorrow night to discover what the letter said. Not being a very patient man, Eddie took a seat in the chair next to Lucy as he pulled out the letter.

"I've been working very hard with Dr. Slater to improve my language skills," Eddie said carefully. "But the letter I received today is in cursive. I'm not experienced with this type of language and was hoping Dr. Slater could help me."

"If ye don't mind, I could read the letter to ya," Lucy said, her Irish accent still very apparent even after her time away from her Irish family. And despite being born into an Irish family, she had long black hair. It was her accent that gave her away each time.

"It may be sensitive, Mrs. Slater. You see, Dr. Slater helped me place an ad in the paper," Eddie explained nervously. Lucy seemed to have understood his meaning because her eyebrows rose as her mouth formed an 'o'.

"I see," she said as she rocked the baby in her arms. "Well, I believe that will be up to ye. I won't tell anyone what the letter says, but the young lady who has written ya might be upset if someone else reads her letter."

"Oh, I didn't think about that," Eddie said, feeling more defeated than before. "Then how am I going to be able to read it?"

Eddie watched Lucy as she rocked in the chair, looking off in the distance as though thinking hard about the situation. "Well, either ye have someone read it to ya, or, ye learn how to read cursive real fast," Lucy said with a smile, as she focused her eyes back on him.

Eddie sighed heavily as he thought about the two options. He could either learn the contents of the letter quickly, but risk upsetting the author of the letter. Or, he could take the time to learn the necessary skills to read it himself.

"Well, I don't want to risk messing up my chance at marriage before I've even begun. I'll learn how to read cursive," Eddie decided, even though he hated to think how long that would take. Lucy smiled at him as though she approved.

"It seems we should get started right away then," Lucy said. Eddie smiled kindly, even though he disliked the idea of having to learn another form of writing. But as he looked down at the letters on the front of the envelope, his motivation was sparked to learn more about the young lady who had taken a chance on him and write him three whole sheets of writing paper.

CHAPTER 4

*A*fter waiting for weeks for a reply from Eddie, Fiona was starting to get discouraged. Since she'd replied to a mail-order-bride ad, she hadn't received any other ads from the agency in the hopes that she would be successful with Eddie. But without receiving a response from the cowboy with a monkey, Fiona reasoned that it was time to inquire with the agency once more to hopefully correspond with someone else.

"Maybe it wasn't meant to be," Fiona mumbled to herself.

"What is that, dear?" Mr. Wilkins spoke up from the head of the table. Fiona had forgotten herself once more and had spoken out loud when she had meant to keep her thoughts to herself. She was surrounded by her father's closest friends, their families, and of course, their eligible sons.

"I was just commenting how wonderful the meal is, and the pleasant company we have this evening," Fiona said with a smile she hoped would be convincing.

"Ah, how nice of you to say," Mr. Wilkins said before turning the conversation back to his business partner.

"Fiona dear, why don't you tell Mr. Leanly how you've been spending your time volunteering at the children's orphanage," Mrs. Wilkins spoke up, startling Fiona since she'd never stepped foot in an orphanage before.

Fiona forced a smile onto her face, willing to play her mother's game. "Indeed, Mr. Leanly," Fiona said, as she turned her eyes to the gentleman that had been purposefully sat next to her in an effort to capture her interest. "The children's orphanage has a lovely plot of land behind the building that they've been using to garden. I help the children with their vegetable garden, teaching them what plants are best to grow this time of year since summer is coming to an end." There were gasps around the table, yet Fiona kept a smile on her face.

"Are you saying, Miss Fiona, that you enjoy gardening? That you're knowledgeable in it?" Mr. Leanly asked in a shocked voice.

"Indeed, sir. I do love to garden. There is a small vegetable garden here that I enjoy cultivating. There is nothing better than tasting the vegetables from your own hard work," Fiona said proudly. If her mother was going to start telling lies about Fiona in front of a room full of socialites, then she was going to make sure she not only embarrassed her parents, but used truths to combat lies. The last thing she'd ever be considered is a liar.

"If I didn't know better, I would say you were a pioneer woman," Mr. Leanly said with a chuckle, causing the others to join him. But as Fiona looked towards her mother, she could see she was not laughing with the others and that her face had turned a shade of red.

"Why thank you for such a lovely compliment, Mr. Leanly," Fiona said, even though her eyes were locked with her mother's. She even laughed with the others when this comment seemed to stir everyone's mirth.

For the rest of the meal, Fiona was left alone. She didn't receive any more encouragement from her parents to speak during the meal, and after her declaration that she manually worked earth to grow vegetables, she instantly became less attractive to every eligible gentleman in the room. But it was no matter to Fiona. She preferred it this way since she would never marry a man who couldn't accept her for who she truly was. And she'd be damned if she was going to be told she couldn't do what she loved by her husband. It was bad enough that she was constantly told what she couldn't do by her parents. She would never tolerate that from her husband.

When the meal had come to an end and the dinner guests had left for the night, Fiona was making her way up the stairs when her mother came walking quickly after her. "You ungracious little girl. How could you embarrass your father and I like that?" she called up to Fiona who had stopped to face her mother. As Fiona stared down at her mother, she squared her shoulders.

"How could you say such a lie about me? I have never been to the children's orphanage. It would be easy to discover that you and I were lying about such a thing. Did you think that one of the families at dinner more than likely volunteers their time there as well? I was not going to lie any more than I needed to," Fiona said in a stern voice.

And before her mother could get in another word, Fiona continued. "Mother, I am not a little girl any longer. I am of age and will not tarnish my reputation any more than you two have already." Fiona then turned and continued up the stairs as her mother continued to call up to her.

"Mr. Crane has asked your father for permission to marry you," Mr. Wilkins then said. Fiona froze on the stairs, her heart beating fast in her chest as she turned around and looked down at her mother, her face red with embarrassment.

"Mr. Crane is twice my age," Fiona replied.

"Yet he's a wealthy man who is sure to make you happy," Mrs. Wilkins shot back.

"Wealth doesn't make a person happy, Mother. Compassion, love, and honesty do," Fiona said as she took a few steps down the stairs towards her mother.

"Those are things of fairytales," Mrs. Wilkins scoffed. "Your father will allow Mr. Crane to marry you if you don't obtain any better suitors."

"But I'm the one who gets to agree to the marriage. Not you, or Father," Fiona said, her anger building.

"Not in this family, you don't. You'll listen to whatever your father tells you to do, and that's final," Mrs. Wilkins said in a high-pitched voice, which was her attempt at yelling at Fiona. She then turned on her heels and walked away quickly. As Fiona stood and watched her mother make her way to Father's study, she knew that the woman would have cross words with her husband. Fiona wasn't going to stick around to hear her parents argue once again. Instead, she turned back around and marched up the stairs, then walked quickly down the hallway until she reached her room.

Once the door was securely locked behind her, Fiona crumbled to her knees as her emotions overtook her. Tears streamed down her face as she sobbed, praying beyond hope that she would find a way out of this mess. She couldn't believe her parents could be so heartless about her future. The image of Mr. Crane rose in her mind. Just the thought made her stomach churn with unease. He was not only much older than her, but also a very round fellow with a sleezy reputation. Even if his income far exceeded her father's, she would never marry him for all the money in the world.

A knock on the door forced Fiona to settle her nerves so no one would hear her sobbing. "It's just me, Miss Fiona," came Mrs. Dickens voice. Fiona quickly wiped her eyes on the back of her hand as she stood and went over to the door. She unlocked it and pulled the door open, eager to get out of the tight-fitting gown her mother had insisted she wear this evening.

"Let's get you ready for bed," Mrs. Dickens said, as another chambermaid came in to assist Fiona. In no time at all, Fiona was stripped of her gown and petticoats and helped into a nightgown. It felt refreshing to not be in so many layers, and after she'd been wiped down with a cool, damp cloth, she felt much better.

"There you go, Miss Fiona. All better," Mrs. Dickens said as she shooed the chambermaid out with Fiona's laundry to tend to. "And if I remember correctly, Mr. Bentley brought up some mail for you," Mrs. Dickens added as she pointed to Fiona's writing desk.

Fiona had been so overcome by her nerves that she hadn't even noticed the letter. But as she looked towards her writing desk, where a candle had been lit and set beside it, she could clearly see a letter postmarked from Montana. She couldn't help but smile as she turned back to Mrs. Dickens.

"Thank you, Mrs. Dickens," Fiona said.

"My pleasure, Miss Fiona. Anything you need, you just let me know," Mrs. Dickens said in a more serious voice. Fiona wondered about the meaning of her words as the woman curtsied and left the room. Fiona locked the door once more before taking a seat at the writing desk.

Fiona picked up the envelope and ran her fingers gently across the printed letters. They were neatly written, and she couldn't help but smile as she looked at her own name. Then, she looked at Eddie Murtaugh's written name and smiled even more. Just when she'd given up hope, she had finally received a letter from him.

Carefully opening the envelope to preserve Eddie's postal address, Fiona pulled out a sheet of writing paper. At first, she was a little disappointed because she'd written such a detailed letter. But she soon reminded herself that a short letter was better than no letter at all. So therefore, she pressed the letter flat to her writing desk as she began to read with excitement.

Dear Miss Fiona Wilkins,

Please forgive me for my late response. Your beautifully written letter took me longer than anticipated to read since I am not familiar with cursive words. But after receiving help from a good friend to learn cursive writing, I then did enjoy your letter, over and over again.

You shared with me so many details about your life in Boston that I can understand why you'd want to leave it all behind. Having been without parents since my brother and I

36

were very young, we've had to work hard for everything we have today. There is a sense of pride that comes from forging your own destiny. And though I know several businessmen and women who work hard, it sounds like if you are born into wealth, then you have a higher chance of taking it for granted.

I'm glad to hear you enjoy gardening. It's a fundamental part of living so far from town. People in our community have to do this for themselves since supplies are limited. Though Mr. Frost keeps a good stock at his mercantile, one can't rely on stagecoaches to make routine stops in our town to deliver more supplies. Therefore, everyone in Spruce Valley maintains their own gardens, and large ones at that.

You asked good questions about Jack, my pet monkey. He's a wild one, for sure, but has a kind side to him as well. He often sleeps at the foot of my bed and will keep me company on long cattle drives. He is liked by many on the ranch, even though he's not allowed in the ranch house after he tore at Mrs. Slater's curtains. He keeps reminding me that he's more a wild animal than a pet. But I wouldn't trade him for the world.

I know you wrote a lot about your life in Boston and how you don't really care for it. I want to reassure you that there are two mail-order-brides here in Spruce Valley, and actually live here on the ranch. Mrs. Slater −Lucy− is a mail-order-bride, and so is my foreman's wife, Martha. So, you'll be in good company here. Lucy and Martha now manage a women's boutique in town, even though they both have small children. I guess times are changing and women are becoming more independent.

Well, it seems I'm rambling now. I look forward to your next letter and promise to respond quicker next time.

Eddie Murtaugh

BY THE TIME Fiona finished reading the letter, she had a wide smile on her face. She read the letter three times over before she pulled out sheets of writing paper and began to write her own response. It was late at night, but she didn't care. She was filled with such excitement to have received Eddie's letter that she wanted to respond right away. She knew it would take some time for Eddie to receive her letter because of the wide distance between them, but she knew the sooner she wrote the letter, the sooner it would arrive.

As Fiona finished her letter and addressed it to Eddie in Spruce Valley, Montana, she sat for a while and looked at the address. She'd have to find a map to discover where Spruce Valley was, and even investigate how to travel there. The idea of traveling by stagecoach sounded dreadful, but perhaps the train went close enough to the small town that she wouldn't have to worry too much about travel arrangements. Fiona was so filled with thoughts that she didn't know how to best organize them, or what type of action she wanted to take. But as she thought about Mr. Crane once more, she knew that no matter what, she was going to leave Boston behind.

CHAPTER 5

*E*ddie was putting his horse in the stable after a long day out under the sun. For the end of summer, it was sure hot. He'd even kept Jack in the bunk house with plenty of water because he was afraid of fatiguing the monkey or allowing him to stay outside for too long. And with the heat, it had also meant hauling extra water from the stream to ensure none of the cattle were getting dehydrated.

"Good work out there today," Gray said, as he came riding into the stables on his stallion.

"Thanks, boss. The heat was killer, but I'm confident the cows have plenty of water 'til tomorrow," Eddie replied as he brushed down his horse, not wanting the beast to feel sweaty with matted hair all night. Not too long after that, Sawyer came riding in with Tom Barker, the other ranch hand.

"Fences are secure, boss. The repairs were pretty minimal and no signs of wildlife," Tom reported as soon as they dismounted.

"Then it seems I'll have good news for the boss man tonight," Gray said with a chuckle, as they all finished bedding down their horses for the night. Then, they made their way into the ranch house for dinner.

"Honey, I'm home!" Gray called as soon as he stepped over the threshold of the ranch house. Eddie chuckled with the others, but Martha was soon crossing the main room to shush him.

"Samuel just fell asleep," Martha chastised her husband, who was quick to close the space between them, wrapping his arms around her and planting a passionate kiss on her lips.

"I'm glad to hear he's well," Gray said when he broke their kiss. Eddie just shook his head as he took a seat at the table. It was another reminder of how badly Eddie wanted something like that in his own life.

"Here's the mail for you, Eddie," Dr. Slater said as he came into the room. He handed Eddie a small pile of letters, which Eddie quickly tucked underneath his leg. He pretended that it was nothing but could feel Sawyer's eyes on him.

As the dinner progressed, Eddie did his best to join in with the conversation where he could. He was eager to look through the letters to see if any of them were interesting. He'd been enjoying his reading and writing lessons with Dr. Slater in the evenings and felt more confident about responding to any possible letters. However, he hadn't received any interesting letters since he'd received Miss Fiona Wilkins' letter.

Eddie was anxious and in a hurry by the time dinner was done. He stuck the letters in his back pocket as he helped clear the dishes and clean up after dinner. He was heading back to the dining table to read his letters and hopefully respond to one, when Sawyer came up to him and spoke in a low voice.

"When are you going to tell me about these letters you keep getting?" Sawyer asked as he narrowed his eyes at Eddie.

Eddie was silent for a moment as he bid goodnight to Tom, Gray, and Martha as they left the house. Dr. Slater was known for retiring to the sitting room, and Lucy had taken Francene to rest for the night. When the coast was clear, Eddie turned his focus back to Sawyer.

"It's nothing yet, Sawyer. I'll let you know when it's serious, though," Eddie said, hoping his answer would please him enough.

"Are you plotting some sort of big move? What do you have in the works?" Sawyer asked as he stepped closer to Eddie.

"Sawyer, it's nothing like that. I enjoy working here at the ranch. Besides, if I was thinking of something else, you'd be the first to know," Eddie said as he looked at his brother with a puzzled expression. Usually Sawyer wasn't this paranoid.

"Yet it seems you've told the Slaters what you're doing," Sawyer said, as he looked over his shoulder where Dr. Slater was sitting in the other room in his favorite wingback chair.

"That's because the Slaters have helped me improve my reading and writing skills. Can't send and receive mail if you can't read and write," Eddie explained.

"But why won't you tell me what's going on?" Sawyer pressed. Eddie stared into his brother's eyes. He could either continue to push his brother away, or he could finally tell him everything.

"Dr. Slater helped me place a mail-order-bride ad in the

papers back East. Mrs. Slater helped me learn cursive so I could read and respond to a letter I had received. And now I have a whole pile to go through, it seems," Eddie said point-blankly. Eddie watched as his brother took the time to process everything he had just said. Then, Sawyer doubled over as laughter riddled his body.

"Shut your trap, Sawyer. You're going to upset Mrs. Slater if you wake the baby," Eddie said as he slapped his brother on the back of the head, shutting him up real fast.

"I'm sorry, Eddie. I thought you were in some sort of financial trouble and that's why you kept getting all those letters," Sawyer said, as he wiped the laughter tears from his eyes.

"Well, now you know the truth. Can I get some peace and quiet to read these letters? It's still hard to read so much," Eddie said, as he sat down at the table and pulled out the pile of letters, setting them before him.

"Do you need any help?" Sawyer asked.

"I don't think so. I figure your reading skills are as miserable as mine," Eddie said as he looked at the address of the first letter, and then started opening it.

"True. I don't read so well, but I can listen to what you think of the letters if you want someone to talk about them with," Sawyer offered, as he sat down at the table across from Eddie.

Eddie observed his brother for a moment. Normally Sawyer would have teased Eddie pretty good about something like this. Especially anything that related to women. But it seemed that Sawyer was being genuine with his offer.

"Sure, why not," Eddie agreed as he opened the first letter.

"Most of them are pretty ridiculous, I'll tell you. Either dull as a doornail, or older women looking for a young man."

Sawyer chuckled as he folded his arms over his chest. "A bunch of old maids hoping to get lucky later in life," he said. Eddie simply nodded his head as he began reading the letter slowly, making sure he could understand it without issue.

"I don't think I could take on four kids right now," Eddie said as he set the letter aside and turned his attention to the next one. When he recognized Fiona's name, he opened the letter as excitement shot through him.

Dear Eddie,

I hope you don't mind that I use your first name. I like to think with each letter we are truly getting to know one another on a first name basis.

The weather in Boston has finally started to cool. It's a blessing since the days have been so dreadfully hot. I'm sure more so in Montana while being outside all the time. But even when it's hot, I do enjoy cultivating my garden or helping Mrs. Dickins with the cooking. I'm sure my parents would love me to learn how to play the piano or spend my time volunteering in the community to attract wealthy gentlemen as suitors, but I thoroughly enjoy creating things with my own hands. I even had Mrs. Dickens show me simple needle work like mending clothes. I take pride in seeing what I can do myself.

My parents have been pressuring more and more to marry. They've even threatened to arrange my marriage. So, since I am now of age, I know that I have the right and privilege to pave my own way in life. I'm not sure why I'm writing to tell you this, but I've always believed that a relationship of any kind should be based on compassion, trust, and honesty. If we are to ever become a match, I want you to know everything there is about me, and what motivates me to take action.

I'm sure I sound like a spoiled brat sometimes, wanting to leave this life of luxury behind and move out West. But you see, I find no pleasure in any of it. Perhaps it's simply because of the type of parents I have, or the pressure of society I currently feel. But I can't help but think that life is simpler in the West. No big cities, no one judging you for your wants and dreams. When I think of possibilities, I think of anywhere but Boston.

Now it seems that I am the one rambling. I've just experienced a dreadful dinner party and my emotions are still running high. But I shall post this letter the day after receiving your last one. I look forward to your next letter to read what has been happening in your life lately. How is Jack doing? Tell me more about the people of Spruce Valley.

Fiona Wilkins

P.S. I've also included a photo of myself that was used in the papers when I was debuted into society this past spring.

As Eddie read the letter slowly, he couldn't help but smile. He found Fiona's letter quite humorous because he couldn't imagine a socialite enjoying things like gardening, cooking, and fixing clothes. But he could understand Fiona's perspective of feeling pride by creating with your own hands. Eddie was proud of the type of work he did and always felt good at the end of the day for having earned a living by doing the best work he could do.

Eddie then took the black and white photo that Fiona had

included with her letter. A faint smile clung to her luscious lips as she looked straight at the camera. Her eyes were mesmerizing, even in the photo. Her hair had been curled and pinned up behind her head, accentuating her long neck. She appeared tall with a slim figure, but not in an unpleasant way. Eddie thought she looked rather delicate, but her letter showcased just how fiery she could be.

Eddie then passed the photo to Sawyer as he folded up the letter and tucked it into his shirt pocket. He planned to respond to Fiona right away, as soon as he read through the rest of the letters.

"Wow. She's definitely not a Western woman," Sawyer replied, as he handed the photo back to Eddie.

"Yes. It's clear that she's from a wealthy family, but she's been very honest and up front about herself and her family. You'll be surprised to know that she can cook, garden, and fix clothes," Eddie said with a chuckle.

"Why in the world would a young lady raised by a prestigious family be interested in those things? Surely she has loads of servants to do that sort of thing?" Sawyer reasoned.

"She explains that she enjoys creating things with her hands, that she takes pride in what she's able to do for herself," Eddie replied. He didn't want to share any intimate details with anyone about Fiona's letters, to respect her privacy. But he was enjoying speaking about her to his brother.

"Well, I guess it's a good thing that she understands how to do some things. She might not have been raised out here in the prairie, but there are plenty of skills that a young woman needs in order to get by," Sawyer said as he stood from the table. "Well, I'm getting some sleep. Tomorrow waits for no man."

Eddie simply nodded in agreement as Sawyer left the ranch house. He felt better having shared his secret with his brother, and talking to him about Fiona also made him feel good. As Eddie looked down at the other letters, he decided it would be best not to even bother with them. He had a good feeling about Fiona and wanted to pursue writing her, even if it meant having to have his ad run again in the paper, at a later time, if things didn't work out. As he looked down at her photo in his hands, Eddie hoped that he'd found the one.

FIONA HAD JUST RETURNED from a tea party with her mother and had made quick work of going straight to her room to avoid any further conversation with the woman, when Mrs. Dickens came into her room. Fiona turned towards her, ready to let her know that she wasn't needed, but she watched as Mrs. Dickens locked the door. Then, the older woman took a letter from her apron pocket and handed it to Fiona.

"Mr. Bentley asked me to hold onto this for you 'til you returned from afternoon tea," Mrs. Dickens explained. Fiona took the letter and saw that it was from Eddie. She smiled as she traced her fingers around the letter. She couldn't wait to read it. But as she looked back up at Mrs. Dickens, she could tell that the woman was worried.

"What is the matter, Mrs. Dickens?" she asked. She set the letter aside, wanting to give the woman her full attention.

"Mr. Crane stopped by while you and your mother were

out. It seems that you'll soon be married," Mrs. Dickens said with tears in her eyes. Fiona was instantly filled with dread as her stomach tightened. She looked away from Mrs. Dickens as tears of her own started to fill her eyes.

"What am I going to do?" Fiona said softly to herself, not intending to direct the question at Mrs. Dickens.

"Don't you want to marry a man such as Mr. Crane?" Mrs. Dickens asked.

Fiona laughed in mockery. "The man is twice my age and quite repulsive. I will never marry such a man," Fiona replied. A faint smile came to Mrs. Dickens' mouth and she couldn't help but smile as well.

"What do you want to do, Miss Fiona?" Mrs. Dickens asked carefully. Fiona looked to the letter on her writing desk and knew that there was a whole world of possibilities waiting for her outside of Boston.

"I will not remain in my parent's home if they are going to force me to marry someone I don't love, let alone respect. If I have to, I'll run away," Fiona said, squaring her shoulders.

"I don't blame you for wanting to go, Miss Fiona. But where would you go?" Mrs. Dickens asked.

"There is a place called Spruce Valley, in Montana. I've heard that it's lovely and a good place for women to choose their own destinies," Fiona explained.

"That's an awfully far place to go," Mrs. Dickens said. "But your parents surely wouldn't think to look for you there."

Fiona nodded her head, thinking that would be true. Then, she wondered just what Mrs. Dickens would do if she did decide to run away. "And if I did flee to Montana, would you tell my parents?" Fiona asked.

Mrs. Dickens smiled kindly at Fiona as the older woman closed the distance between them and took Fiona's hands in hers. "I've been with you since the day you were born, Miss Fiona. I've watched you grow up into a very fine woman that any mother would be proud to have. And though I am not your real mother, I like to think I've cared for you as such. And as a motherly figure in your life, I want what is best for you. I will miss you dearly, but I like to think that you'd write me when you got settled," Mrs. Dickens said with fresh tears in her eyes.

"Oh, Mrs. Dickens. How could I ever leave you behind? Surely you'd want to come with me?" Fiona asked as she fought back the tears that threatened to spill from her eyes.

"No, I am far too old to be setting off on any adventures. You must go on this trip alone and make a way for yourself. Just tell people you're a married woman returning home from visiting your family in the East. I bet I could even find you a ring to wear if you needed it," Mrs. Dickens said as she let go of Fiona's hands and wiped away her tears.

"Now then. It seems we have much to do to get you ready to travel. And I'm afraid we don't have much time to do so. If I heard correctly, the wedding itself should take place in a fortnight," Mrs. Dickens said.

Fiona was shocked to discover that her wedding would be so soon when her parents hadn't even told her, nor had she agreed to such a thing. Fiona was burning with anger as she considered it all. How could her parents expect her to truly go through with the wedding when she would never agree to such a thing?

"I'm not sure how to get started, Mrs. Dickens. Surely my

parents would discover my plans if I tried to shop for the trip, or even make my own traveling arrangements?" Fiona queried, worried she could actually escape before the day of the wedding.

"Don't worry, my dear. I'll get everything settled for you. Mr. Wilkins won't even know a thing 'til you are long gone," Mrs. Dickens said with a pleasing smile. "But for now, you better keep out of sight. I'm sure your parents will want to tell you the news yourself. Try to act surprised and not upset too much. I promise you, I won't let you marry Mr. Crane."

"Oh, thank you dearly, Mrs. Dickens. I don't know how I would have survived this long without you," Fiona said before Mrs. Dickens unlocked the door and stepped out into the hallway. Fiona quickly locked it after her and sat down at her writing desk. She was overcome with emotions as she looked down at Eddie's letter. She desperately wanted to open it, but her mind was racing so fast concerning her own situation, that it took her some time to calm down before she could open the letter and read it.

Dear Fiona,

Thank you for writing your last letter in print. It made it much easier to read and I appreciate your consideration. I'm sorry to hear that your parents are pressuring you so much into marrying. I can't imagine that and can only admit that there is much about your lifestyle that I may have a hard time understanding. Life here in the West is very different because everyone must grow or raise their own food and make what they can. There are only a few businesses here, so we have to make do with what we have.

This time next year, I hope to start building my own home.

I enjoy the bunkhouse and the comradery of the other ranch hands, but one day I want to be able to sit out front on my own front porch and watch the sun set. I want a place I can feel excited about returning to each day. I don't know if I ever want to start my own ranch, but I do know I want my own plot of land. It doesn't need to be very big, just big enough for me and my future family.

I'm only twenty-five, but I do know what I want in life. I think my brother Sawyer is starting to think the same way. He was so paranoid about why I was receiving so many letters. I was at first embarrassed to tell him that I put in an ad for a mail-order-bride, but getting to talk to him about it, and about you, made me feel really good. I like to think that I'm making good choices for my future and that includes taking chances.

Thank you for the photo you sent with your letter. I can honestly say you're a beautiful woman. Any man would be honored to have you as their wife. I wish I had a photo to send back to you, but I've never had the chance to be photographed. Perhaps that's something else I can look forward to in the future as well.

I hope this letter finds you well, and I'm glad to hear the weather in Boston is cooling down. Things are still hot here in Spruce Valley, but I'm sure fall weather is right around the corner. I look forward to your next letter.

Eddie Murtaugh

CHAPTER 6

The train whistle blew, signaling the train would soon be leaving the station. Fiona stood on the platform, her hands intertwined with Mrs. Dickens as they looked at each other with tear-filled eyes. It had been a week since Mrs. Dickens had told Fiona the news about her arranged marriage and they were able to put into place this plan for Fiona to flee Boston. Mrs. Dickens had made all the travel arrangements for Fiona. It had taken some time to purchase the proper traveling clothes and things Fiona would need to get settled in Spruce Valley, but Fiona was now ready to make the trip.

"I knew the day would come when I would have to say goodbye to you," Mrs. Dickens said in a shaky voice. "There's writing paper in your trunk. Make sure to write to me as soon as you are settled, and not a moment later."

"I will, Mrs. Dickens. I will let you know that I am well and safe, and hopefully I'll be writing to let you know that I am happily married to a man I actually love," Fiona said with a smile as tears streamed down her face. She didn't realize how much she loved the older woman until she had to say goodbye.

The whistle blew a final time, signaling its departure. Fiona quickly let go of Mrs. Dickens hands and stepped up onto the train as it started to move. She stood on the narrow stairs, waving to the woman as the train started to pull away. She was filled with so much pain in her chest to be leaving her behind, but since today was the day that her mother planned to take her to get fitted for her wedding dress, she knew she couldn't wait any longer.

As the platform disappeared from sight, Fiona finally made her way into the passenger car. In the hopes of trying to fit in and not stand out as a socialite, Fiona's ticket was for a common seat instead of an entire cabin to herself. With a limited amount of funds, she'd have to make smart decisions moving forward.

The further the train pulled away from Boston, the more excited Fiona became. She was able to eventually settle her nerves and clear her face of tears as the sun started to rise. It was a brand-new day, and the first of many days until she would reach Spruce Valley. She would be able to take the train all the way to Montana, but eventually she'd have to rent a stagecoach to take her straight to Spruce Valley. And even when she got there, she wasn't certain what she would do when she arrived or how she would get in touch with Eddie. She knew that he worked on Dr. Slater's ranch, so she figured that would be enough information to help her locate him.

Fiona tried to picture Eddie in her mind as the train made

its way. She had taken a seat next to the window and was able to watch the scenery come alive with the morning sun. Fiona wondered if Eddie being tall meant he was taller than her, which she hoped he was, even though she was a tall woman herself. She even wondered what it would be like to go on a real date with him instead of having to attend a dinner party and have their meeting arranged by her parents.

Fiona rubbed the golden band on her wedding finger, a tool Mrs. Dickens assured would help her stay out of trouble. She didn't want to attract any unwanted attention by traveling alone. Appearing as though she was a married woman would help others hopefully respect her. But as she looked down at the wedding band, she wondered what it would be like to be married to a cowboy like Eddie.

But all that Fiona knew for sure was that the further and faster the train made its way away from Boston, the happier she would be. Shortly after hearing the news from Mrs. Dickens, her mother and father had summoned her into the drawing room to explain to her that Mr. Crane had asked for Fiona's hand in marriage. That not only had her father accepted the offer, but also the business investment that Mr. Crane was willing to donate to his company. She'd been appalled to have been sold in such a way but had done well to keep her emotions under control. She didn't let her parents see her disapproval, knowing that Mrs. Dickens would help her escape. Instead, she had accepted the news with grace before returning to her room.

For the next few days after speaking with her parents, Fiona had done her best to avoid them as much as possible and spoke very little at dinner. There was even one point when her father asked if she was feeling well because she'd become very lifeless around the house.

"Yes, Father. I am healthy," Fiona had replied, without even looking at her father as she enjoyed the butternut squash soup that she'd helped Mrs. Dickens prepare that day.

While she'd been avoiding her parents, she instead had spent every available moment with Mrs. Dickens. The older woman was doing her best to prepare Fiona for living as a pioneer. Fiona had to quickly learn to cook basics such as bread, rolls, and meats. Though she often became flustered when cooking, Fiona had never given up. She was doing her best to learn as much as she could in such a small amount of time.

During the evenings, Fiona would sometimes think of the things she would miss the most. Mrs. Dickens had explained that indoor plumbing wasn't common in the West. Fiona had learned this from her Western novels but hadn't really put much thought to it. Now, however, she was facing all sorts of things that she hadn't considered until planning on physically leaving her home. She knew it would be difficult to adjust to a completely different lifestyle, but she knew that anything would be better than being forced to marry Mr. Crane.

After an hour of traveling by train, Fiona was starting to feel rather relaxed. She didn't mind the constant rocking of the train as it made its way. She rather enjoyed seeing the forests and countryside, wondering if any of it would be like Montana. She'd never traveled outside of Boston before and thought that everything she was seeing was like traveling to a completely different world. She imagined that this is what every heroine in her books had felt when they began their journey. Fiona couldn't wait to see what the train would pass by next.

EDDIE WAS HEADED into town with a package from Lucy to be delivered to the boutique. She'd finished adjusting a dress for Mayor Stavros after taking it home to finish, and now wanted to make sure the Mayor had it as soon as she needed it. Eddie was more than happy to run this errand since things seemed to be going smoothly at the ranch. Just yesterday, he'd been in town with the wagon to pick up food and other supplies for the ranch. He hadn't received a letter from Fiona, so he was hoping today would give him another chance to stop by the mercantile to see if any new mail had come in on today's stagecoach.

As Eddie made his way into town with Jack resting on his shoulder, he made quick work of going straight to the women's boutique to drop off the dress. As he dismounted in front of the store, which was situated along with the other businesses on the main street, he handed Jack a date in the hopes of keeping him occupied so he could quickly drop off the gown, and then head over to Frost's to check on the mail.

"Good afternoon, Eddie," Martha said happily as Eddie walked into the store. He didn't quite enjoy the boutique because it always smelled overly flowery. But he reasoned that it was the type of thing that women liked. He set the package down carefully on the counter.

"Mrs. Slater sent me into town with the Mayor's gown. Said she finished it last night and needed to have it brought into town as soon as I could get it here. So off I went," Eddie said with a chuckle. Jack then barred his teeth and screeched at Martha as he tried to laugh along with his master. The sound startled the other ladies in the boutique and Eddie quickly reached up and pulled Jack down from his shoulder and cuddled him in his arms.

"Thank you, Eddie. That was very kind of you. I hope you have a good day now," Martha said quickly as she escorted Eddie out of the store.

"I'm sorry Jack frightened your customers," Eddie said softly once they were outside the store. "Jack was just laughing."

"I know, Eddie, but most don't understand the sound a monkey makes when it laughs. You two go on with your business and get back to the ranch. I'm sure everyone would agree that Jack is cute, but he's still an animal," Martha said in parting. She then quickly returned to her boutique and began chatting with the customers.

Eddie sighed as he placed Jack back on his shoulder and gave him another date. "Come on, Jack. We best be quick," Eddie said in a melancholy voice. Seeming to understand his master, Jack hugged the side of Eddie's face, causing him to chuckle.

"Don't worry, I still love you," Eddie said as he stroked the monkey's soft fur before pulling himself back up into the saddle of his gelding and making his way further into town.

Frost's mercantile was a center place for Spruce Valley. It not only served as the general store, but also the stagecoach depot and a café in the back called The Eatery. Mr. Frost and his wife were great people and always made patrons feel welcomed. And now that the mercantile housed a telegram machine, it had become quite a busy place.

As Eddie stepped into the mercantile, he quickly received a few puzzled looks with Jack hanging onto his shoulder. It was well known that Eddie now owned the British man's monkey. With Spruce Valley being a very small town, Eddie knew that everyone already knew. But knowing and seeing seemed to be two completely different things. To Eddie, it seemed that Jack scared most people away. And since Eddie often left Jack at home with either Sawyer or Tom, he rarely brought Jack into the mercantile either. But with the other ranch hands busy today, Eddie had little other choice.

"Afternoon, Eddie. Afternoon, Jack," said Mr. Frost from the front counter. Eddie made his way quickly there to hopefully pick up the mail and go before Jack had a chance to do anything naughty.

"Afternoon, Mr. Frost. I've just come in to see if there is any mail, and perhaps see what kind of dried fruit you might have in stock," Eddie explained as he raised one hand around Jack, in case the monkey decided to act up. Thankfully, Jack took it as a sign of affection and wrapped his monkey arms around Eddie's head.

Mr. Frost chuckled as he pulled out the mailbox and started flipping through it. "One letter for Mr. Eddie Murtaugh," Mr. Frost said as he pulled out the letter and handed it to Eddie. Eddie quickly pocketed it as he pulled a few coins from his pocket. "And let me get you a bag of dates. I know how much Jack loves them."

"You would be correct, Mr. Frost. He loves them so much

he thinks they're treats since he normally just eats bugs," Eddie explained.

"My, my. I would have never known. I bet he keeps the bunkhouse clean of any pesky things, then," Mr. Frost said as he filled a small sack full of dates.

"That he does, sir," Eddie replied as he looked around the general store. There seemed to be a good number of people in the store today, and they all appeared to be keeping one eye on Jack.

"Here you go, Eddie," Mr. Frost said as he handed him the sack of dates. Eddie set the change down on the counter before he accepted the dates.

"Thank you kindly, Mr. Frost. You have a good day now," Eddie said as he turned to leave. But then he came face-to-face with one of the women he used to run around with. Not that he was the only one who often did.

"Well, well. If it isn't Eddie Murtaugh, the handsome Murtaugh brother," Nicky said as she licked her lips. "Oh, and what a cute pet." As she reached out to touch Jack, Eddie took a step back.

"He doesn't like to be touched by strangers, Nicky. Now if you don't mind, I have to be getting back to Dr. Slater's ranch," Eddie said as he tried to step around Nicky, but she placed her hands on her hips and used her elbows to block his way.

"So, you're working as one of Dr. Slater's ranch hands now? I never pictured you to be a hard-working type of fellow. I thought you and your brother liked to chase bad guys with Sheriff Ryder?" Nicky said in a sultry voice.

"We've both put that type of life behind us now, Nicky.

We'll help out Sheriff Ryder any time, but I like where I am at now and would very much like to get back to work, if you don't mind stepping aside," Eddie said as he narrowed his eyes at Nicky, catching her off guard. She stepped aside as she shook her head at him.

"I always thought you were polite towards women," Nicky said as she raised her voice. Not wanting any trouble, Eddie simply gave her one hard look before making his way to the door.

Eddie sighed heavily as he stomped towards his horse. He wasn't proud of the fact that he'd slept around with a few women in town and prayed that it wouldn't come back to haunt him one day. But if Nicky was going to act this way towards him in the future, he worried about it hurting his chances of marrying in the future.

As Eddie made his way out of town at a canter, he gave Jack a date from the sack to help keep him calm as they made their way back to the ranch. Jack ate the date with his tail wrapped securely around Eddie's neck. It didn't hurt Eddie but instead allowed Eddie to receive some form of comfort from the monkey. He had known the moment after seeing Jack in Handy's that the monkey was special, and he was glad that Jack was proving him right from time to time.

Once he was out of town, Eddie slowed his horse to a walk so he could retrieve the letter he'd received. As he pulled it out of his back pocket and looked at the address, he was pleased to see that it was from Fiona. But as he looked at the postmark, he was a bit concerned to see that it had been posted in Indiana. Eddie quickly opened the letter and began reading as fast as he could.

Dear Eddie,

My letter will no doubt come as a surprise. By the time you receive this letter, I will most likely be much further in my journey than Indiana. I left Boston a few days ago after the news came to me that I had been put into an arranged marriage with a man twice my age. My beloved housekeeper, Mrs. Dickens, helped me arrange all my traveling plans and the things I may need while living out West. You see, I've run away from home and I'm now making my way to Spruce Valley. I don't want you to feel pressured, because this is my choice. But I hope we can meet in person and see how our relationship will develop from there.

I'm excited to meet everyone you've written about in Spruce Valley. I'm sure to arrive by stagecoach and get to meet Mr. Frost first, like you've mentioned in a previous letter. I'll be sure to book a room at the Honeywell Inn, and then come to see you from there. I look forward to meeting you, and to creating a new life for myself in Spruce Valley. I know it will be hard to adapt to living in the West, but I know that any future I create for myself will be better than being married to Mr. Crane.

I don't have many skills, but I feel prepared for living as a pioneer woman. I'm sure as I travel, I can think deeply about my abilities and what I may be able to do for employment. If you know of anyone hiring, I look forward to learning about it once I arrive. I'm determined, and I think that's the best thing I can offer someone right now.

Well then, I shall be seeing you after a bit.
Fiona Wilkins

. . .

AS EDDIE FOLDED the letter and stuffed it back into his pocket, he turned his horse around and started back towards town. If Fiona would be arriving in the foreseeable future, then he would have to let a few people know so that when she was spotted, she could be properly directed.

When Eddie made it back to town, he made his way straight to the Sheriff's Office. He and Sheriff Josh Ryder had been good friends ever since childhood. Josh's father had taught both Eddie and Sawyer how to shoot rifles and pistols, and was one of the reasons Josh often called after the brothers any time he needed back up when tracking down criminals. Sometimes Eddie missed the thrill of chasing someone down with Josh, but the peace he felt when on cattle drives couldn't be beat.

After dismounting and tying the reins to the front post, Eddie took Jack inside the building that Josh used for work. As soon as he stepped through the door, Josh startled awake from where he'd fallen asleep at his desk. Eddie couldn't help but chuckle as he took a seat across from Josh's desk. Josh tried to smooth back his brown hair.

"Morning, Sheriff," Eddie said with a smile. Jack jumped off his shoulder and plopped onto the desk, his eyes spotting Josh's sheriff badge pinned to his vest.

"Yeah, yeah," Josh said as he took off the badge and handed it to Jack. The monkey liked shiny things and held it in his hands to inspect it. "What brings you by, Eddie?"

"Well, there is a certain young lady making her way to Spruce Valley that I want you to be on the watch for. Her name is Fiona Wilkins," Eddie said. That bit of news seemed to wake Josh as he looked wide-eyed at Eddie.

"I didn't know you knew anyone outside of Spruce Valley," Josh said with a smile.

"Well, as I'm sure you can deduce, she's a mail-order-bride. She's coming early after having run away from her parents in Boston who had just arranged for her to marry a man twice her age," Eddie explained.

"Sounds a bit dramatic to me, Eddie. Sure you want to get mixed up in some rich family's problems?" Josh asked.

"From her letters, I can tell that Fiona is a fierce woman who isn't willing to let anyone tell her what to do. Sounds like the perfect woman for me," Eddie said with a smile, as Jack started to tap the badge against the desk.

"Alright there, Jack. Give me back the badge," Josh said as he extended his hand towards the monkey. Jack barred his teeth and screeched before jumping back up onto Eddie's shoulder. "Hey now, it isn't funny."

"Actually, it's hilarious," Eddie said with a chuckle as he traded a date for the badge with Jack, and then handed the badge back to Josh. "Anyways, what has you so exhausted?"

"Well, there's been a run of train robberies from here to Massachusetts. Every sheriff anywhere close to a train station has been telegrammed and warned about the robbers' identity. I've been putting my brain to work, gathering as much information as I can, and thank God we have a telegram machine here in town now, or I would have never known about it," Josh explained as he rubbed is eyes. "I think it's time for some coffee from The Eatery."

"Sure looks like you could use some," Eddie said as he stood with the Sheriff. "And I best be getting back to the ranch. I didn't expect to be gone this long, but as soon as I received Fiona's letter, I just knew I needed to let someone else in town know about it."

"No problem, Eddie. If I get word of her arrival, I'll let you know," Josh said as he came around the desk and shook hands with him. As the two left the Sheriff's Office, they parted ways. And with Jack securely back on his shoulder, Eddie mounted his horse and made his way back towards the ranch once more.

CHAPTER 7

*B*y the time Eddie made it back to the ranch, he was brimming with excitement. It had finally hit him that someday soon, he would be meeting Fiona. He tried to figure out in his head how many more days it might take for Fiona to reach Spruce Valley, since the closest train station was two days away by stagecoach. But eventually Eddie stopped trying to figure it out and simply felt more excited than he had in years.

When he got back to the ranch, he made quick work of letting Mrs. Slater know that the task was finished and that the dress had been delivered to the boutique. He also couldn't help but share the good news with her that Fiona was traveling to Spruce Valley.

"Oh my word, what good news! I'm sorry to hear that she was forced to choose between marrying and leavin', but sometimes a woman has very little choice when yer born into wealth. Anyways, I'm just so glad for you, Eddie. I'll talk to

Sam about having Fiona stay here when she makes it to town," Mrs. Slater said happily.

"Oh no, I couldn't put that kind of burden on you and Dr. Slater. Fiona already knows that there's the Honeywell Inn in town," Eddie said. He was glad that Mrs. Slater could share in his enthusiasm but didn't want his boss to go out of his way for him.

"Well, we both know how much I dislike the Honeywell Inn, even though Bill is a great man and runs a good business," Mrs. Slater said with a sigh. "I'm going to talk to Sam about it tonight and we'll let ye know."

"I appreciate the consideration, Mrs. Slater. I better get back out there though," Eddie said as he dipped his head and quickly left the ranch house before Jack had a chance to cause any trouble.

After making sure Jack was secure in the bunkhouse (since his little furry friend had been out in the sun all day already), Eddie mounted his horse and took off into the pasture, excited to share the news with everyone else.

"No kidding!" Sawyer said in reply when Eddie found him. Gray and Tom pushed the cattle to another pasture that had grown tall grasses.

"Just received her letter today. I have no idea when she'll be arriving, but I made sure to let Josh know since he stays in town and always knows what is happening," Eddie explained.

"That's a good idea. Josh won't let her wander around aimlessly," Sawyer agreed.

"No kidding. The moment Martha arrived in town, Josh practically told everyone. Sam made it home just in time for me to get dressed and head into town to surprise her for dinner," Gray said, shaking his head as the others laughed.

"I happened to mention it to Mrs. Slater as well when I got back to the ranch. She said she's going to talk to Dr. Slater about allowing Fiona to stay with them. I think that would help her feel more at home," Eddie said. He was concerned about Fiona and how she was currently feeling since she had felt pressured to leave her home so unexpectedly. He only hoped that she was enjoying her travels and wouldn't run into any trouble.

"Well, if for some reason the boss man isn't keen to the idea, I'm sure Martha wouldn't mind having Fiona stay with us," Gray said as he kept an eye on the cattle. Eddie was surprised by the offer but nodded his head in agreement.

"Thanks, Gray," Eddie said as they began to focus on the work at hand.

As Sawyer and Eddie moved around to the other side of the herd to ensure that none of the cattle were disappearing between the two pastures, Eddie could tell that Sawyer wanted to say something. But he didn't speak up until they were a bit further away from the other two.

"So, what do you think about a city girl coming all the way out here to avoid getting married?" Sawyer asked Eddie in a soft voice as they rode side-by-side.

"I do have my worries about it, Sawyer. She wasn't raised in this type of lifestyle and might realize that living with her parents is a better deal than this. Perhaps she'll get all the way here and want to go home and marry a rich man when she realizes how harsh the West can be," Eddie said as he voiced his fears.

"That's understandable, Eddie. I mean, look at Mrs. Slater. She came from a big city, too, but she adapted with time. Though, Dr. Slater is better off than most. And Greta does come to help Mrs. Slater from time-to-time with the house-work. Hell, even Gray has been cooking more and more meals with the woman working at the boutique while raising two young children," Sawyer said. Sawyer was always the more logical of the two of them, and he appreciated his perspective on the matter.

"I think it will come down to her passion and motivation to be out here. I really do hope none of my fears come true, but I think I'll have to keep a level head about all of this. After all, she may get here and we may not even like each other in person," Eddie said with a shrug of his shoulders.

"I'm glad you're thinking about this matter, Eddie. But also, don't lose hope. It's okay to get excited about meeting a woman," Sawyer said with a smirk.

"Yeah. The first woman I actually want to date and not just enjoy between the sheets," Eddie said with a chuckle.

"You're the better brother for sure, Eddie," Sawyer said, causing them both to laugh loudly.

"Hey, you two! Knock it off!" Gray called over the cattle, causing the Murtaugh brothers to quiet down and get back to work. But Eddie couldn't stop feeling excited inside.

FIONA WAS FEELING UTTERLY DREADFUL. After a week and a half of traveling by train, she was racking her brain to try to remember why any of the heroines in the novels she'd read had described traveling by train to be a thrilling experience. For the first few days, Fiona had learned a lot about train travel. First, the train stopped often, sometimes giving passengers a chance for a short break and to stretch their legs. But Fiona was so afraid of not reaching the train in time before it left again that she rarely left.

Furthermore, she found that after a while, looking at the scenery became boring. She continued to see the same things over and over again and she was certain that the entire world was covered in forest with areas of civilization mixed into it. Fiona had tried to enjoy the one novel she'd brought with her, but found that it no longer appealed to her. She was seeing firsthand what it was like to go on an adventure. And sometimes it was quite unpleasant.

The food on the train was often stale, salty, or simply uneatable. When she got up the courage, she would scurry off the train during stops to find some fresh bread and cheese to enjoy. But the further away the train traveled from major cities, the less variety and fresh foods Fiona found.

Fiona had gotten used to relieving herself on the train, though it was always a scary moment because the train was always moving and shaking. When fresh water was available, she tried to soak her handkerchief in some and wipe her skin down the best she could in the changing room. She found that it was easier to wear the same two traveling gowns she'd brought with her. But as the train neared Montana, she decided to wear one of her nicer gowns that she'd decided to keep as a memory to her old life.

Though traveling by train had been odious from time to time, the thing Fiona enjoyed the most was getting to know all the people in her compartment. All sorts of people from various social classes were traveling out West for one reason or another. Some were returning West after visiting family in the East, much like the story she told everyone she met. Others were on their first trip out West in hopes of striking it rich in a gold mine, or starting their own homestead. Fiona always enjoyed hearing the stories that were motivating, that detailed why they were leaving it all behind and taking a risk in an unknown land. These stories were very similar to what she was feeling and currently experiencing.

Just two days left on the train before Fiona would be able to finally disembark and start the rest of her journey by stagecoach. The hours seemed to stretch out and Fiona was feeling rather restless. Even in one of her nicer gowns that smelled of home, Fiona couldn't seem to get comfortable. She had walked up and down the train cart a few times and tried to strike up conversations with a few people she'd come to know, but alas, she became rather bored. Even with the scenery having changed from forest to open fields, little seemed to entertain Fiona at this point. That is, until the train was suddenly stopped.

"My word, why has the train come to a stop?" said an older man, sticking his head out into the aisle as though he could see through the many passenger cars to the front engine.

"Do you think there is something wrong with the engine?" queried the woman next to him. There were various whispers of concern until shouts could be heard from towards the front of the train. When gun fire was heard next, everyone slunk back into their seats and became very quiet.

"Just do whatever they tell you to," whispered the woman

sitting across from her. She held a young boy in her arms and was using her hands to shield his eyes and ears. Fiona went to ask who the woman was referring to when the front of the train car was opened suddenly, and a tall man with a bandana tied around his face stepped through with a pistol held high.

"Toss your valuables in the aisle and no one will get hurt!" the man yelled, his voice muffled by the way the bandana covered his mouth. A cowboy hat covered his head, only allowing his eyes to be seen on his face.

Everyone in the car started to throw their things into the aisle. Purses, watches, wallets, money, and jewelry were quickly flung in hopes of not being shot in return. Fiona tossed her purse in with the fray before pulling off her wedding band. She went to throw it but couldn't possibly part with Mrs. Dickens' present to her. So instead, she tucked it up her sleeve in the hopes of it not being discovered.

"You there. Surely someone dressed as fine as you still have more to donate," the man said to Fiona as he pointed his gun at her. She was instantly shocked into silence as she stared at the gun, her heart beating fast in her chest. All Fiona could manage to do was shake her head rapidly in hopes of conveying that she had nothing else on her.

"Come now, don't give me any trouble. Best to just give it up," the man said as he grabbed Fiona by the arm and pulled her to her feet, so he could check where she'd been sitting. But as the man continued to hold onto her arm in a rough manner, instinct took ahold of Fiona and she lashed out at the man, smacking him in the face.

"Take your hands off me! I've already given you my purse with all my precious things in it. Take the things and get on with you," Fiona shouted as she stepped away from the man. The robber glared at Fiona as he rubbed the spot on his face where he'd been struck.

Another robber then came onto the train with a large burlap sack in his hand and started to quickly pick up everything that had been tossed into the aisle. But when he saw his partner standing there with his gun pointed at a woman, he spoke up. "Hey, what's going on?" This man was shorter than the other and seemed to be experienced at his task as he continued to collect the items and toss them into the sack.

"She's just being feisty, is all," the robber with the gun said as he continued to glare at Fiona.

"Well, she's a woman. What do you expect?" the robber on the floor said as he picked and scooped up every valuable thing.

"I'll have you know that I'm the daughter of Mr. Mathew Wilkins of Boston. And once he hears how you robbed me, I'll ensure both of you are hanged for assaulting me," Fiona said in her anger. Her face turned red as she stared back at the man who held a gun at her. She was frustrated and tired of traveling by train, and the little money she had left was being taken by someone else. But as both robbers came to stand in front of Fiona, she suddenly felt very stupid for opening her mouth.

"So, yer a daughter of a rich father, are you? Seems to me that you are the most valuable thing on this whole train, then," the man with the gun said. The way his eyes wrinkled told Fiona he was smiling under his bandana.

"Been a while since we've had a hostage. A pretty thing like her would be fun to have around," the smaller man said. Then, without warning, both men quickly grabbed Fiona's arms and started pulling her down the aisle towards the open door.

"Take your hands off me! Let go this instant! Help! Someone help me!" Fiona shouted, as she pulled and fought against the two men. She tried to become a dead weight in their hands, going limp and trying to curl up on the floor, but they continued to wrestle with her until she was being pulled down the narrow steps to the ground. Furthermore, it shocked Fiona to the core that no one was coming to her rescue.

Tears were streaming down Fiona's face as she was pulled to her feet and quickly bound around her hands. A handkerchief was tied around her head and mouth to gag her from talking. Her kidnappers dragged her over to a group of horses that was being tended to by a man Fiona assumed was a criminal as well. The other robbers in the posse were quickly descending the train with similar burlap sacks that seemed to be full to the brim. As the others gathered around Fiona, the two that had kidnapped her quickly explained the situation.

"Great job," said a man with a very deep voice. "We'll return to camp and send someone into town to post a telegram to Mr. Wilkins. Something tells me we're all about to become very rich." There were whoops and cheers to the news from the other robbers. Then they all saddled up. Fiona was pushed up into a saddle and forced to ride with her legs on either side of the saddle. She turned red in the face as her stocking legs became apparent for the men to see. Never having been on a horse before, Fiona gripped onto the saddle horn with all her strength as the reins were taken up by her tall kidnapper.

Fiona held on for dear life as the horses were put into a fast trot across the open plains and away from the train. The rhythm of the running horse was so foreign to Fiona that she was afraid that at any moment she'd be thrown off the beast. She tried to rock her hips with the momentum of the horse, but it wasn't long before her rear end was becoming very sore and she did not know how much longer she could take such a beating.

In the distance, she could hear the train's whistle once more, signaling that it was departing. The posse of robbers was already long gone, to the point that no one could possibly save her now. She tried to keep her emotions under wraps because she was mostly concentrating on not falling off the horse. She squeezed her legs each the side of the horse, doing her best to stay on the saddle all the while gripping the saddle horn. But she couldn't help but think what would possibly happen to her next.

After a while, a thick wood line came into view, and the robbers slowed the horses to a canter, leading them one by one through a narrow parting in the trees. It was like being trans-ported into a whole other world as the open plains faded away and the thick forest of North Dakota quickly surrounded them. Fiona was trying to focus on her breathing, taking deep breaths trying not to hyperventilate as the sun seemed to disappear. It was much darker and cooler in the forest as Fiona listened to the sounds of chirping birds. She could see squir-rels and chipmunks running along tree branches and up and down tree trunks.

If it had been under any other circumstance, Fiona would have found the forest very majestic. But even though she was taking in different sounds, sights, and smells of the earthy forest, her mind was still focused on the robbers in front and behind her. The horses followed a narrow trail that seemed to be well-known by them. Fiona moved her hips to the movement of the horse, trying to follow the motion of the saddle. Her body was so tense that she started to silently pray that soon they would be able to dismount, even if that meant the next horrible part of her abduction would commence.

Fiona didn't know what would become of her, or if her father would even send money for her after she'd run away from home. She was scolding herself horribly for speaking up on the train and wished she'd just followed the advice of the woman that sat across from her. She could be on the train right now if she'd just tossed the gold wedding band onto the floor with the other precious things and turned away from the robbers. But no. She'd opened her mouth and let her emotions get the best of her. And now she would probably pay for doing such a ridiculous thing.

And the worst part of it all seemed to be the fact that she'd probably never get to meet Eddie in person, if she did get out of this mess alive.

CHAPTER 8

*E*ddie was laughing with the others at dinner time as Martha teased Gray about being over protective of Samuel during a picnic at lunch that day. His gut hurt from laughing so much, and he had to cover his mouth with his hand in order to settle his laughter.

"My goodness. Sam is the same way. We were riding into town to have Francene's medical checkup at the clinic and he insisted on holding her the whole way," Mrs. Slater said, as another round of laughter sounded about. Everyone found it hilarious that the two fathers were so protective of their children that at first, no one heard someone knocking on the door.

"I'll go get it," Tom spoke up when the knocking sounded again. He quickly got up from the table to answer the door and Eddie returned to eating his food. He wanted to hurry up and be done so he could get back to Jack in the bunkhouse. The other night, Jack had gotten into the cupboards and tossed all the extra plates and cups onto the ground. And, not liking to keep Jack cooped up in his room, he wanted to go check on the pet monkey as quickly as possible.

"Evening, folks," Sheriff Ryder said as he came into the dining room. "Sorry to bother you all, but Eddie, I need a moment with you."

Eddie looked up from his plate with concern as he focused on his friend. He quickly finished chewing the food in his mouth to take a sip of water before standing from the table to follow the Sheriff into the other room.

"Everything okay, Josh?" Eddie asked in a soft voice. He was nervous because Josh had only asked to talk to him and not Sawyer.

"Eddie, you remember me mentioning those train robbers a few days ago?" Josh said as he rubbed his chin. It seemed that Josh hadn't shaved for days and had started to grow a shadow of a beard. As Eddie really looked at Josh, he could tell the man was exhausted.

"Yeah, I remember," Eddie replied.

"I just got a telegram from Frost. It's from a sheriff in North Dakota, right on the territory line of Montana. It explains that another west-bound train was robbed," Josh explained.

Eddie was silent for a moment as he tried to process what Josh was really saying. "You think it could be the same train that Miss Fiona is riding on?" Eddie asked.

"I'm sure of it, Eddie. The telegram explained that a young girl was taken hostage after she threatened the robbers, because her father is Mr. Wilkins of Boston. The passengers who witnessed the kidnapping have explained that the robbers plan to hold her as a hostage," Josh said softly.

Eddie was so taken back by the news that he was silent for several minutes. He just stared at Josh, waiting to wake up from this nightmare. But after he pinched himself hard in the leg, he realized that he wasn't sleeping, and that Fiona was in real trouble.

"Her family should be notified right away," Eddie said, as his mind started to spin towards taking some sort of action. His thoughts were split between imagining what Fiona was going through and how he was going to save her.

"They've already been sent several telegrams," Josh reassured.

"Where in North Dakota was the first telegram sent from?" Eddie asked, mentally making a list of all the supplies he'd want for this rescue.

"Medora. That's the station the train pulled into next after being robbed," Josh explained.

"Then that's where I'll go first. From there, I should be able to find something that will lead me to where the robbers are keeping Fiona," Eddie said, walking out of the room to let the others know that he had to leave immediately. But Josh grabbed him by the collar of his shirt and tightened his grip on him, forcing Eddie to stop.

"Now hold on there, lover boy. You can't just go running off into the night without a solid plan," Josh said as he forced Eddie to look at him. "Plus, you're going to need back up."

"And who's going to back me up?" Eddie asked.

"I am, dummy," Sawyer said as he stepped into the room. "I've been listening to the whole thing in the hallway."

"But what about the ranch? We can't both lose our jobs," Eddie replied as Josh let go of him.

"But we also can't allow a young woman to die in vain. She was coming out here to meet you and we have a responsibility towards her," Sawyer said in a stern voice.

Eddie stood for a moment before he nodded his head. He agreed that he felt responsible for Fiona, since it was his letter that told her of Spruce Valley, influencing her to come here when she needed to flee her home. He just hated the idea of losing their jobs over it. Even if they did rescue Fiona, what kind of life could he offer her if he didn't have solid employment? Reconciling that was a problem he'd have to address later, Eddie made his way into the dining room to tell the others.

"Sorry to do this, Dr. Slater, but Sawyer and I have to head out. The train Miss Fiona was traveling on has been robbed, and she's been taken as a hostage," Eddie said. He knew there was no point mincing his words and the ladies gasped in shock at the news.

"You can't just leave, Murtaugh. You need to have some sort of plan," Gray spoke up.

"That's what I told them," Josh said as he came into the dining room after the brothers.

"We'll figure it out as we go. But we have to get to North Dakota as quickly as possible," Sawyer said.

"You're going to need more than just gun hands against an unknown number of robbers," Gray retorted.

"And it wouldn't hurt to have a doctor with you," Dr. Slater added.

"And probably a good tracker," Martha spoke up then.

Eddie was dumbfounded as he looked to everyone in the room. He couldn't believe what they were implying. He felt so overwhelmed with support that tears started to pool in his eyes.

"Yeah, I think that is a great idea," Eddie said in a shaky voice.

"I'll get dinner cleaned up," Tom said as he stood from the table. "I'll try to pack some supplies for the road."

"I'm going to get the children put to bed. Martha, ye might as well stay here for the time bein'," Mrs. Slater said as she stood from the table with Francene on her one hip, and collected Samuel and rested him on her other hip. She toddled from the room to get the little ones ready for bed.

"Martha and I will ride over to the Crow Tribe camp and speak with Bright Star. We will try to convince him to come with us as well," Gray said, as he helped Martha to her feet.

"And I'll start getting my medical bag ready, along with the guns," Dr. Slater stated. Eddie was in awe as everyone was quick to help and take action. So many people were moving in different directions that at first, Eddie didn't know which way he should go.

"Gray, I'll join you and Martha. Bright Star should hear the news from me, after all," Eddie said as he followed the couple onto the front porch. "Sawyer, make sure to check up on Jack!" His words were followed by a grumble from his brother.

"Well, come on then," Gray gestured over his shoulder, as they made quick haste of getting to the barn and hooking up the horses to the wagon. Thankful for a full moon to guide their way, Gray snapped the reins, sending the two horses into a fast pace as Martha sat next to him on the wagon's board bench and Eddie sat in the back. As the night wind whipped his face, he prayed that Fiona was alive and well.

SEVERAL FIRES still burned brightly as Gray, Martha, and Eddie entered the Crow Indian camp. They were quickly halted by the sentinels, but once they saw the families faces, they let the wagon pass on into camp. The news of their arrival quickly spread through the camp, and soon Bright Star and his two sons, Running Bear and Sky Bird, were coming to greet them as they climbed down from the wagon.

"It is good to see my favorite redhead," Bright Star said to Martha in way of greeting. She laughed as his two sons grunted in response.

"It is good to see you as well, Bright Star. But I'm afraid that our visit is not one of leisure," Martha said regretfully.

"Is Samuel Jenkins well?" Bright Star asked quickly, concern on his face.

Gray chuckled as he shook his head. "No, Bright Star. The little one is well. I'm sure because of your great blessing for the children this past spring," Gray assured.

"Bright Star," Eddie spoke up. "We've come to ask for your help. You see, there is a young woman who was riding on a train to come to Spruce Valley. We are meant to meet one another in hopes of marrying. But her train was robbed, and she has been taken hostage. I plan to ride straight to

North Dakota to hopefully locate her and bring her to safety."

Bright Star looked at Eddie with much concern on his face. Then, he looked to his two sons. "My sons, I feel compelled to help this young woman, much like I did for Martha Jenkins last year. Would you two accompany me, or do you wish to stay with our tribe?" Bright Star asked his sons. Eddie felt relief that Bright Star would agree to come with them, but feared what his sons would say as they regarded one another.

"The tribe needs able men to help prepare for the journey south for the winter. We will leave to follow the buffalo in just a few short weeks," Running Bear said as he focused on his father.

"I agree, Father. I know that the tribe will not remain in Montana for much longer as summer fades to fall. It will be hard enough losing one great warrior to this cause," Sky Bird said in agreement with his brother.

Bright Star nodded his head as he looked at Eddie for a moment. "Nonetheless," he spoke up. "I must go and do this thing. I feel the Great Spirt would have me go."

"Very well, Father," Running Bear said in a soft voice. "Let us prepare you for this journey, then."

"Good. I shall join you at the Slater Ranch before the rising sun. Go and sleep, for tomorrow morning we shall ride hard," Bright Star said in a voice that held great authority. Gray, Martha, and Eddie nodded their heads as Bright Star turned and made his way back through camp with his sons close by. Without any further words, they all climbed back into the wagon and Gray guided the horses around and back towards the main road.

"I don't think I'm going to be able to sleep tonight," Eddie spoke up from the back of the wagon.

"Well, you're going to have to try. You're no good to anyone if you don't get some rest," Gray said over his shoulder, as he steered the two horses back towards the ranch through the dark. Even though no one could see him, Eddie nodded his head. He tried to put his mind to focusing on everything he would need for the journey and how fast he could gather supplies together tonight so they could all leave in the morning. But his heart pounded in his chest as he thought about Fiona and what type of circumstance she might possibly be in.

"Please, Lord, watch over Fiona," Eddie whispered into the night as he looked up into the sky, watching the stars intently.

It had been three days since Fiona had been taken hostage from the train. The robbers had taken her deep into the woods where their camp was situated between several rocky formations. There was a small gap in-between the rock wall that allowed enough room for their horses, their bedrolls, and a central firepit. After arriving at this camp, Fiona had been lowered down from the horse and taken over to a post on the far side of the camp between the tallest parts of the rock formation. Her bound hands had then been tied to the post and the gag in her mouth removed. It was a relief to have the handkerchief off her head and mouth, but as she looked around the camp, she knew that escaping would be almost impossible.

As Fiona watched the others around her move about, she saw how they hid the burlap sacks deep into pits in the ground that were easily covered up by a wooden door and then disguised by fall leaves and branches. The horses had a place where they were tied up to other hitching posts and fed from feed bags and a central water trough. There was a small shed in the back of the clearing that looked to be a place to store supplies. Here, the short man who had been collecting everyone's valuables from the train, went to start gathering things to cook with.

Fiona watched everything going on around her as the five robbers all seemed to have some sort of job to do now that they were back at camp. Fiona didn't dare say anything else that might get her into trouble. She knew now to keep quiet and simply look for a way out of this mess.

In all the days they'd been at camp, none of the robbers had removed their bandanas or cowboy hats while they were around her. She reasoned that this had something to do with the fact that they were trying to keep their identity from her. It was this little fact that gave her hope that one day soon she would be released. But she hadn't heard any of them speak about sending a telegram to her father, or if a reply had been received. In fact, any time the robbers did speak, it was in hushed voices, so Fiona couldn't hear anything they were saying most of the time.

Three times a day, Fiona was brought a small cup of water and some sort of gruel to eat. It tasted rather horrible, but Fiona knew that she needed to keep up her strength and therefore needed to eat whatever was given to her. This was often the time of day when the robbers would begin to tease her.

"I bet a princess such as yerself has never eaten poor man's food before," the tall robber laughed, causing the others to laugh with him.

"That's right. I bet all that rich people eat is fish eggs and snails," another said, their laughter continuing.

"That's a good one, Smitty," said the short one, as he spooned more gruel on a plate for the others. But the group quickly went quiet as they stared at him. Even from a distance, Fiona could see the way they glared at the shortest robber, especially the man the robber had called Smitty.

"Ah, I'm sorry," the short one said in a soft voice as he looked between Fiona and Smitty. But Fiona quickly turned her eyes to the ground and looked at her slippered feet as though she hadn't heard anything. They all chastised the short man for several minutes, taking the focus off her as she quickly ate her food and finished drinking her water.

And so the days passed in this manner. She spoke very little and watched everything that happened around her. At night, she hardly slept. And during the day, she sweated in the heat. Still being dressed in her finest gown and several petticoats, she felt much warmer than she would have if she'd remained in her traveling gown. But there was nothing to be done of it now. At night she was thankful for the layers, because the air would turn very cold and she was never given a blanket to keep warm.

The only time she was unbound from the post was when she needed to relieve herself. One of the robbers would come over to her, untie her, and lead her out of the camp and into a small grove of trees. There, she had to hike up her skirts and carefully take care of her business. She already smelled of sweat and dirt. She didn't want to add to her smell and therefore was careful of what she did.

During the day, sometimes she would stand and move her legs in hopes of staying active. She knew that sitting all the time would do her no good. It also gave her something to do while she watched the robbers in the camp. Sometimes, some of the men would leave with the items they'd stolen in the burlap sacks. She assumed they were trying to sell or trade the items in exchange for more supplies. And even though the shortest robber always had enough to cook with, his food always tasted of ash and dirt. It was awful, but filling enough.

"Boss, when are we going to move on?" complained the tallest robber. Fiona focused in on the two men, wanting to know as much as she could about their current situation.

"Not until we hear back from the mister. If he doesn't agree to pay the two-thousand dollars, then we'll dump and run," the boss of the robbers said in his deep, dark voice.

"The longer we stay, the easier it will be to get caught," another robber said in an uneasy voice.

"I'm not stupid, ya hear me?! I've been running robberies and taking hostages since you were still a wee little thing. If you want out, go on then," the boss man said in a loud voice, causing the others to observe the two of them carefully. In Fiona's opinion, things were getting tense at camp. Pairs were talking in soft whispers and often everyone was keeping an eye on the boss man. Fiona wasn't quite sure what was going on, but she had a horrible feeling in her stomach.

Fiona silently prayed all day and night, hoping that no matter what happened next, she'd at least be free from this hell. She was starting to regret ever leaving Boston and wished she'd just stood up to her parents when they tried to marry her off. Perhaps if she'd taken to finding a decent husband more seriously, she would at least have been able to choose her husband instead of having to settle for Mr. Crane. As Fiona kept her eyes locked on the robbers around her, she feared not only for her life, but whatever future she could have once all of this was over.

CHAPTER 9

The open plains shot past Eddie as he sat on the bench of the covered wagon, the dirt road stretching far beyond and behind him. Jack, for the most part, stayed perched on Eddie's right shoulder, his monkey tail wrapped around his shoulders. And sometimes he'd sit on his lap and try to position himself inside Eddie's vest. Eddie was thankful for the comfort of the small animal close to his chest as he tried to keep his nerves under wraps.

The wagon rumbled along the road with four other horses running beside it. Dr. Slater, Gray, Josh, and Bright Star rode Indian ponies that Bright Star had brought from the camp for them to use, insisting that they would be faster than any of the horses they owned at the ranch. The only downside was that they all had to learn how to ride bareback very quickly. Having been on the road for two days already, it helped that Dr. Slater, Gray, and Josh quickly learned the best way to ride the Indian ponies so they could make it to North Dakota without needing to rest for very long.

With Eddie and Sawyer taking turns leading the team of horses that pulled the wagon with supplies, they were able to travel as quickly as possible on horseback. With every new morning, Eddie was motivated once again to reach Medora in North Dakota, and start gathering clues as to where Fiona might currently be held captive. He'd never traveled this far from Spruce Valley, but he kept reminding himself that this adventure would be worth it if it resulted in finding Fiona safe and sound.

"Alright, fellas," Josh said as they started to near Medora near nightfall on their third day of traveling. They slowed down to a canter so they could talk amongst themselves. As they neared the town, they knew they would be seeing other people more frequently on the road.

"I'm going to head into town with Dr. Slater and Eddie. I'll meet with the local sheriff and we'll collect all the information we can. Gray, Bright Star, and Sawyer, I want you guys to find a place to set up camp for the night. We don't want to spook anyone since we have Bright Star with us. Gray, once camp is set up, come into town and let us know," Josh said in his authoritative voice. Bright Star chuckled and took no offence to Josh's plan. Their group knew that not everyone accepted Indians as civilized people, unlike those in Spruce Valley had come to do.

"Switch me spots then, Eddie," Gray said as he pulled his Indian pony to a stop by tugging on his mane. Eddie then stopped the wagon and encouraged Jack to stay with Sawyer.

He knew that having the monkey in town would only cause problems.

"Hey there, little buddy," Sawyer said as he took Jack and put him on his shoulder. Eddie couldn't help but smirk as he saw Sawyer warming up to Jack. Then, when Eddie was ready, he quickly hopped onto the pony like Bright Star had taught them, while Gray climbed up onto the wagon and picked up the reins.

"We're all set then. We'll see you all in a bit," Dr. Slater said with a nod, as he tapped his heals into his pony and set off with Josh and Eddie.

Eddie was brimming with excitement and uneasiness as they made their way into the town. He'd been looking forward to this moment for the last three days as his body was filled with worry for Fiona. He couldn't wait to get to hear what the local sheriff had to say about the situation and if any progress had been made in finding Fiona. He just hoped that they would be met with friendliness as they sought out the sheriff.

"Looks bigger than Spruce Valley, that's for sure," Josh said as they came onto the main street of the town. Businesses lined the street as locals walked up and down the boardwalk. In the distance, they could see the train station that was currently empty. Eddie figured that the railroad had brought a lot of business to Medora and thought something like that would really benefit Spruce Valley. But for now, all that Eddie was concerned about was finding the sheriff.

"I reckon we'll find answers in there," Dr. Slater said as he pointed to a wooden door that had a giant sheriff's symbol painted in yellow on the front of it.

"Don't ever let me do something like that," Josh said with

a sigh as they made their way over to what looked to be the sheriff's office. As they dismounted from the Indian ponies, they had to tie rope around the beasts' necks and secure them to the hitching post in order to keep them situated. Then, they walked up to the door as Josh knocked heavily on it.

"Come in!" called a man from inside. Josh opened the door for them and stepped in first. As Eddie brought up the rear, he closed the door behind him and looked around the office. It looked rather modern with whitewashed walls, polished wooden floors, and a mirror hanging on the wall. It was more a sitting room than a sheriff's office.

"Good day, gentlemen," said an older man as he stood from his desk and moved around it with a bright smile on his face. "Have you come for my autograph?"

Eddie refrained from laughing as Josh moved aside his duster to show the man his sheriff's badge.

"Sheriff Miller, my name is Sheriff Josh Ryder. My deputies and I have just come from Spruce Valley in Montana after receiving your telegram about the train robbery and the young lady that was taken hostage," Josh explained. The older man looked puzzled as he looked at Josh, and then at Dr. Slater and Eddie.

"Well then, why have you come here?" Sheriff Miller asked.

"Because Miss Fiona Wilkins is my bride-to-be," Eddie spoke up. It wasn't completely true, but it was one of the reasons why Miss Fiona had started to make her way to Spruce Valley.

"Forgive me, young man, but Mr. Wilkins never telegrammed me anything about a fiancé all the way out here,"

Sheriff Miller said with a critical eye on Eddie.

"That is because Miss Fiona didn't share with her parents that she was becoming a mail-order-bride. It was the reason she was on the train heading to Montana," Eddie further explained.

"I see, then. Well. We haven't heard anything from the robbers, yet Mr. Wilkins has let me know that he received their telegram about a ransom amount and a time frame. But that's all I know," Sheriff Miller said as he went around his desk once more and took a seat in the chair. Josh, Dr. Slater, and Eddie all gave each other a look of uncertainty before Josh turned back to the other sheriff.

"Sheriff Miller, what is the ransom amount and when is the deadline?" Josh asked.

"The robbers have asked for two-thousand dollars to be delivered by next Monday," Sheriff Miller replied in a grave voice.

"But that's only three days away!" Eddie exclaimed.

"Indeed, son. That's why I'm a little surprised you are all here because there has been no word from Mr. Wilkins on whether or not he's on his way to pay the ransom," Sheriff Miller said.

"But what are you doing about it all?" Dr. Slater asked quickly.

"What can be done? These robbers have been pillaging trains for months. No one has been able to find them, and if Mr. Wilkins isn't willing to pay the ransom, then what can I do about it?" Sheriff Miller said with a shrug of his shoulders. Eddie was brimming with anger as he glared at the older man.

"How far back was the attack on the railroad?" Josh asked.

By the way his jaw was clenching, Eddie could tell that the man was furious as well.

"About three miles east along the railroad," Sheriff Miller said. Then, Josh turned and began to leave the building without another word. "Hey! Where are you going now?" the sheriff asked.

"We're going to go rescue Miss Fiona, like you should have done already," Josh spat at the older sheriff before opening the door so hard that it slapped against the building, scaring a few people who had been walking by. Dr. Slater and Eddie followed quickly after Josh as he untied his pony and mounted. He then turned the pony in the direction they had come, forcing Dr. Slater and Josh to make haste.

"What's the plan, Josh?" Eddie asked as they caught up with him.

"We wait to regroup with Gray once he comes into town and leads us back to camp. In the morning, we'll follow the train tracks to where the scene of the attack was, and hopefully there, Bright Star can lead us to the robber's camp," Josh explained.

Eddie rode silently with the others back out of town. As they followed the road once more, they eventually happened upon Gray as the sun was setting. After filling him in on the situation, Gray shook his head in disgust.

"I can't believe the sheriff hasn't done anything. Sounds like he's a bit showy but doesn't actually do the work," Gray said as he began to lead them away from the road and into a nearby tree line.

"No kidding. Makes me appreciate you even more," Eddie said to Josh.

"Don't thank me yet, Eddie. We still have a lot of work ahead of us, and a very short time to find Miss Fiona," Josh said in a serious voice. Eddie simply nodded his head, knowing what the sheriff said was very true.

Once they'd reached town, Eddie had been so optimistic that they'd have a bigger lead on where to go next. But it seemed that their adventure was only just getting started.

It was early in the morning when Fiona awoke. She was freezing from another cool night without any protection from the elements. She was in a tight ball on the ground as she tried her best to keep warmth in her body. But she felt rather cold and stiff this morning, and as she sat up, she felt lightheaded and stuffy. She could instantly tell that she had some sort of sickness and would not recover properly from being left out in the woods without any protection.

As Fiona's head eventually cleared, she looked about her and realized that the group of robbers were still asleep. Smoke drifted up from the firepit in the center of the men, but it was clear that no one had risen to put more wood on the fire. As Fiona's eyes moved from each one of the sleeping robbers, she watched their chests rise and fall in a deep slumber. Thinking that she needed to escape before she died out in the middle of nowhere, she started to pull at the ties that bound her.

Having been tied up for almost a week now, the cords had become loose around her wrists. She pulled at them without making any sound as she wiggled her wrists through the ties. Fiona breathed a sigh of relief as her left hand pulled free and she used it to pull her other hand through. For a moment, Fiona rubbed her wrists together as she looked towards the sleeping robbers once more. Fiona knew that she couldn't wait much longer, so she stood up onto shaky feet, hiked up her skirts, and started to move around the outer parts of the camp to the narrow opening in the rocks.

As Fiona moved slowly, doing her best not to make a sound, she kept shifting her eyes between the narrow opening and the robbers, who were still asleep. She prayed fervently that none of them would wake so she could be gone long before the first one arose. Fiona didn't know where she would go after she escaped, but she reasoned that anywhere was better than here. And with the gold ring still hidden in her dress sleeve, she figured it would fetch her enough money to make her way back home.

Fiona's heart was pounding so hard that she could hear her blood rushing through her ears. She was terrified yet determined to escape. And as she made it to the narrow rock opening, she turned her back on the camp and began to make her way out. However, she didn't make it far before she tripped over a line of rope she hadn't seen in the foliage of the forest. The moment her foot made contact with the rope, a rattle of empty bottles sounded from above.

"Someone's coming!" shouted one of the robbers, causing fright to fill Fiona's body. She grabbed her skirts and pulled them up high as she moved over the hidden rope and took off into the forest. Fiona had no idea where she was running, but with fear running through her veins, she simply knew that she needed to get as far away from the camp as possible. She wound her way through the trees, hoping they would provide her enough cover to not be seen.

"She went this way!" called someone from behind her, causing a spike of fear to be wedged into her heart. She now knew that they had discovered she'd escaped, and would be tracking her immediately.

Hoping to lose them in the forest, Fiona started running more to her right. She figured that going in a straight line would be too obvious, so she adjusted her course and ran for her life. Her heart pounded in her chest from the exhaustion of sprinting and her breath came in hard gasps as she tried to breathe in air. Sweat covered her body from running and from the sickness that had set in, shivering throughout the night. Now, her body felt like it was on fire as she ran for all that she was worth.

Yet despite her best efforts, she cried out in surprise as one of the robbers cut her off on horseback, forcing her to stop and fall back as she tried to turn and run the other way. She tried to scramble to her feet, but the robber was faster. As the man approached her, she tried to kick him away, but her body was very weak by now.

"Oh no you don't, Miss Wilkins. You don't go free till daddy pays up," came the dark voice of the leader. Fiona began to cry then as the man made quick work of binding her wrists once more, the rope feeling tighter than before. "But I must say, you have more fight in you than I would have ever imagined," he laughed as he pulled Fiona back onto her feet. He then tied another rope to her wrists before pulling himself up into his saddle, using the additional rope to pull her behind him.

Fiona felt hopeless and exhausted as she was forced to walk all the way back to camp. As time passed, she realized just how far she'd been able to run, and it taught her just how large the forest was. Even with the distance she'd been able to gain from the camp, she'd still not seen a way out of the forest.

Tears streamed down Fiona's face as she was pulled back into camp. Even with their faces covered by bandanas, she could see the hatred in the robbers' eyes. She knew she should be afraid of how they would treat her from now on, but she was so tired and exhausted that she didn't have any more strength to be fearful.

The moment she was tied back to the hitching post, Fiona collapsed to the ground. Her chest rose and fell as she tried to catch her breath. Her body ached all over, and though she felt hot and sweaty, she began to shiver from exhaustion.

"She doesn't look so good, boss," said the tallest robber as they all crowded around her. Fiona closed her eyes, trying to block them all out from her reality. No matter how hard she tried to breathe, it felt like her lungs weren't receiving enough oxygen. She even reasoned that she would soon die from having tried to run as hard as she did.

"Serves her right for trying to escape. If she dies, she dies," said the boss in his dark voice. Fiona listened as the robbers all walked away, some mumbling to themselves.

It was a long time before Fiona was able to breath easily. She lay on the ground on her side, her arms shielding her face from the rising sun. She kept her eyes closed, knowing that there wasn't anything for her to really see at the camp. Fiona listened to the coming and goings of the robbers but paid them no attention. Even when one came to give her the morning meal, Fiona didn't bother with it. She was too exhausted to even raise her head and drink the water.

Eventually, Fiona blissfully passed out. She reasoned a fever had taken hold of her.

CHAPTER 10

The moment the sun had peeked over the horizon, Eddie was instantly awake. He lifted his head from his bedroll to see a fire burning in the central pit that had been constructed last night. His eyes traveled to see that Bright Star was already awake and tending to the fire.

As Eddie moved out from his bedroll, Jack uncurled himself from the bottom and made his way out as well. Eddie smirked as he watched the monkey stretch and move around the fire as though he was warming himself. Then, he scurried back to Eddie for his morning meal.

"I never knew that anything like Jack existed. He reminds me of a small child," Bright Star said in a soft voice. The others were still sleeping, and though Eddie was eager to get moving this morning, he didn't want to disrupt their much needed rest.

"The moment I saw him, I just knew I wanted him for a pet," Eddie replied as he picked Jack up and set him on his shoulder whilst the monkey enjoyed pieces of dried fruit. Eddie made quick work of rolling up his bedroll and sticking it in the wagon before taking care of his business. Once he came back to the fire pit, Jack was eating his second date, and Eddie started on making some sort of breakfast.

"May I hold Jack?" Bright Star asked as he extended an arm towards the monkey.

"If he'll come to you," Eddie replied as he shifted over towards the Indian. He moved his right shoulder towards Bright Star, trying to encourage Jack to move off his shoulder and towards the Indian's extended arm. Jack made a few clicking noises with his mouth as he turned his head to the side and looked at Bright Star. When the Indian returned the noises, Jack found this fascinating as he unwound his tail from Eddie and hopped over to Bright Star. Eddie chuckled as he watched the Indian and the monkey exchange clicking sounds. Eddie started to prepare breakfast.

"It's too early for such racket," Josh said, rolling over from where he was sleeping on the ground, looking over towards Bright Star and Jack.

A chuckle rose up from Gray as the man continued to lay on his back with his eyes closed. "That is because you don't have children yet, Josh. When the little ones come, you'll be awake at all hours of the night," Gray said as he raised his arms over his head and stretched. Slowly, everyone woke and rolled up their bedding before joining at the fire. By then, Eddie had finished frying some lard in a cast-iron skillet to cook a few eggs and salt biscuits.

"Not bad, Eddie," Gray said as he dug into his food. Eddie

knew that was a compliment coming from a man who often cooked.

"I learned from the best," Eddie retorted as they all focused on their food. Gray had taught him much about cooking over a fire when they'd been working on a cattle drive last fall. Eddie wouldn't say he was a good cook, but he could make edible food that filled the belly.

The moment they were finished eating and had everything cleaned and put away in the wagon, it was time to get ready to move out. Eddie approached Bright Star then, thinking it was time to retrieve Jack, who surprisingly had been on his best behavior whilst with the Indian.

"Come on, Jack," Eddie called after using his signaling whistle for the monkey. But as Eddie watched Jack, the monkey remained on the Indian's shoulder.

"Do you mind if Jack travels with me today, Eddie Murtaugh?" Bright Star asked with a kind smile. Eddie was surprised that Jack hadn't come to him when called, and that the Indian was taking a liking to his monkey. He wasn't sure how he felt about it, but for now he saw no harm in it, since their main focus was finding Miss Fiona.

"I don't mind, Bright Star," Eddie decided. He nodded to the Indian before pulling himself up into the driver's seat of the wagon.

"Alright folks. Here's the plan," Josh announced. "We'll ride out to the railroad and follow the tracks east for about three miles. Everyone, be on the lookout for any signs of something out of place. The littlest detail can be a huge lead. Once we make it to the place where the robbery took place, we'll fan out and look for signs of their escape." Josh spoke in a loud enough voice that everyone could hear him. There were words of agreement as Dr. Slater doused the fire with a bucket of water before tossing the bucket in the back of the wagon and mounting his own pony.

When they were all set, they followed Josh's lead. It took a while to leave the forest behind, and once they reached open plains once more, they set off at a fast pace. Dust and dirt filled the air as the ponies raced forward with the wagon trailing behind. Eventually, Eddie had to put on a bandana to shield his face from most of the dust.

As they continued, eventually they came up to the train tracks. They turned their progress east, following the tracks away from the town. With every passing minute, Eddie was filled with more determination to succeed. From time to time, his eyes would spy the terrain ahead and scan the horizon. The path the train took covered mostly open plains, but to the right of them was a large forest that seemed to go on forever. As Eddie took in the scenery, he prayed that Fiona was somewhere close.

Eddie slowed down the wagon as Josh raised his hand in the air, signaling for all of them to stop. When they came to a halt, he slid off the back of his pony quickly and dropped to the ground, closely observing the ground with his fingers. A second later, Bright Star was at his side with Jack still placed firmly on his shoulder. Eddie watched as the monkey held onto Bright Star's long black hair as the Indian moved with speed and agility.

"I can see scattered footprints here, Bright Star," Josh spoke up. Eddie watched as Bright Star nodded and began to follow the footprints away from the train tracks.

"Someone was dragged through the dirt and appeared to put up some sort of fight," Bright Star said as he walked. "And here there was a group of horses."

Eddie tied the reins to the board of the wagon before jumping off to quickly follow Bright Star. He looked to the ground to where the Indian was pointing to see several hoof prints in the dry ground. Though it had been over a week since Fiona had been kidnapped, the lack of rain had allowed the prints to remain in the brush. Eddie followed the direction of the hoof prints and eventually his eyes rose to the forest in the distance.

"Seems to me that they took off into the forest over there," Eddie said as he pointed towards the tree line.

"Very good, Eddie Murtaugh," Bright Star said with a smile. Jack screeched and bared his teeth as he laughed in his own way. This surprised Bright Star and he looked at the monkey with concern. Eddie couldn't help but laugh as he shook his head.

"That's Jack's laugh, Bright Star. He thinks you were telling a joke by the way you smiled," Eddie explained. Once Bright Star understood, he laughed as well. Yet this only caused Jack to laugh in return, and soon the two were laughing at each other.

"Alright, that's enough monkey business, you two. Bright Star, I'm putting you in the lead. Let's follow these tracks and see if we can't find Miss Fiona before sundown," Josh said as he shook his head and went back to his pony. Eventually Bright Star's mirth subsided, and everyone readied once more to move forward.

The thought of getting to see Miss Fiona by sundown set

fire to Eddie's determination. With his pistol on his hip, Eddie was ready for anything. He and Sawyer had aided Josh several times in the past, and just like Sawyer had said before, there was a certain thrill about chasing down bad guys.

"Are you ready for this?" Sawyer asked with a smile as Eddie climbed back up onto the wagon.

"Absolutely," Eddie replied with a grin, right before he snapped the reins and sent the horses forward with a jolt. Together as a group, they raced into the forest as Bright Star led them forward.

FIONA FELL into a world of dizziness and uncertainty. Her body was riddled with pains and aches, her skin felt like it was on fire and she continued to shiver as though freezing. For what seemed like days, Fiona was mostly unconscious, always dreaming of trying to run very far away from the robbers but never seeming to get very far. Yet when she was awake, she kept her eyes closed because she was too dizzy to open her eyes. Her breathing always came in short gasps, as though she truly had been running while she slept. At one point, she felt someone help her up into a seating position and coaxed her to drink some water. But the moment she was laid down again, she quickly passed out once more.

It was in this state that Fiona began to dream of something different. She heard gun fire ringing in her ears, followed by the sound of shouting, chaos, and screams of agony. Fiona felt like she could feel fear all around her as she only focused on freeing her hands and running away once more. But whatever sickness had befallen her had a tight grip on her body. She no longer had the energy to run and simply lay on the ground.

Fiona reasoned that she would die soon. The thought brought tears to her eyes as shouts sounded all around her. She heard the frightened neighs from the horses and truly felt sorry for them. But she thought that soon it would all be over. She would fade away into death and no longer feel the pain that riddled her body. She regretted never seeing her parents again, and more so she hated herself for ever running away from the safety of her home. She even wished she'd married Mr. Crane so she didn't need to experience this painful death.

When everything went silent around her, Fiona figured she'd died. There was silence and blackness all around her, even as she continued to struggle to breathe. Then, she felt the bounds around her hands cut free and arms encircle her as she was pulled from the ground and carried away. Fiona risked all logic and forced herself to open her eyes. For a brief moment, she saw that she was being carried by a man with light brown hair and bright blue eyes. He looked down into her eyes. She smiled, thinking she was being carried away by the most beautiful angel in Heaven. Feeling relief like never before, Fiona closed her eyes once more and drifted away.

IT HAD TAKEN some time to follow the horse tracks through the dense forest. But when a large formation rose in front of them, Josh had signaled for them to stop and dismount. After tethering their ponies and horses, they had crept close together to speak softly.

"I bet you everything I'm worth that their camp is inside of that," Josh whispered. Bright Star nodded in agreement as he pointed towards it.

"We need to move in carefully," Dr. Slater spoke up. "We have no idea how many are there or how much gun power they have. My biggest concern is safety at this moment."

"And don't forget traps," Sawyer spoke up. "If they are all in there, there must be something out here to warn them of people coming up onto them. They might have a scout or something else to warn them."

"Good point, Sawyer. We need to approach slowly and carefully. Keep your eyes on the ground for possible traps and ropes," Josh said as he nodded his head.

"I shall go ahead and scout out the area. I have the eyes for seeing hidden things," Bright Star said in a confident voice. Josh simply nodded his head, but before Bright Star could move away, Eddie quickly spoke up.

"Shouldn't you leave Jack behind?" Eddie asked softly.

Bright Star looked at him and smiled. "Don't worry, Eddie Murtaugh. Jack is a good boy and will not be any trouble," Bright Star replied. Eddie forced himself to nod his head, even though he was worried about moving forward with Jack. The monkey was a comfort, but also quite unpredictable.

Eddie watched with the others as Bright Star crept forward. At one point, he removed a large knife from its sheath on his leg. The blade glinted in the few rays of sunlight that passed through the tree's canopy. Eddie could tell that it wasn't just any old knife. He assumed that it had been designed for the purpose of taking lives quickly.

Eddie felt like he was sitting on pins and needles as he

waited for Bright Star to return. He wasn't sure how long they had waited, but he could feel sweat collecting on his forehead. At one point, he lifted his arm and wiped the sweat from his brow as he tried to settle his nerves. He was anxious to move forward and see for himself if there was anything within the rock formation.

Eventually, Bright Star returned to their group with a serious expression upon his face. "There are indeed people inside the rock formation. Upon a closer look, I could spot a campfire and several men inside. I counted at least five of them," Bright Star explained.

"And what about Miss Fiona?" Eddie quickly asked.

Bright Star nodded his head again, but his eyes were dark with concern. "I did spot a young lady through the narrow opening. She was lying on the ground and did not look very well," Bright Star explained in a grim voice. Fear instantly pierced Eddie's chest, so much so that he even raised his hand to grip the front of his shirt.

"We need to move quickly then," Dr. Slater spoke up. "We can't wait much longer if she needs medical attention."

"Agreed," Gray said as he pulled his pistol from the holster at his side. Josh did the same, signaling for the others to prepare themselves. Eddie was itching to move as he pulled out his gun and rested his trigger finger on the side of the barrel, gripping the handle firmly.

"There are many trip ropes along the way. Be mindful to step over them or we'll lose the element of surprise," Bright Star warned as he gripped his knife and turned back towards the robbers' camp. As a group, they all crept towards the rock formation slowly. As they neared various trip ropes, Bright

Star pointed them out and they all made their way over them cautiously.

When they came to the narrow passage into the rock formation, Eddie was able to see just a glimpse of the camp. He could see a group of horses and smoke rising from a camp-fire. Josh raised his hand for all of them to see and when he counted to three with his fingers, they all stood and rushed the camp.

Time seemed to slow in an instant as they all ran through the narrow opening, their guns aimed at the first person they came across. Shouts of surprise filled the air as the robbers were quick to collect their guns and try to take aim. But with the surprise ambush, they were able to fire their guns before the robbers could defend themselves. Cries of pain followed the sounds of gun fire as they were quick to disarm the robbers and begin tying them up.

When the gun smoke settled, Eddie felt relief that none of their team had been shot after one particular robber had been able to get a few bullets out before he was taken down. Though none of the robbers seemed to have been killed, it looked like a few of them had serious gunshot wounds.

"I'll get them patched up and then we'll head back to town," Dr. Slater said as he stood and ran for the wagon to collect his medical bag.

As he left, Eddie seemed to remember why they were all here. The thrill of the gunfight faded, and Eddie quickly looked around for Miss Fiona. Just like Bright Star had described, he found Miss Fiona on the far side of the camp. Her hands were tied together and a lead rope connected her hands to a hitching post. She lay unconscious on her side with her arms stretched out in front of her.

"Bright Star! Your knife!" Eddie called. The Indian was to his side in a moment. Jack was still on his shoulder but had been gripping his hair tightly in fear. Bright Star quickly cut the rope around her wrists and Eddie pulled it apart. A moment later, Eddie pulled Miss Fiona into his arms and quickly took her away from the camp.

As Eddie carried Miss Fiona towards the wagon, he could tell that something wasn't right. Her skin was hot to the touch and sweat was all over her skin. Yet, as he held her close to his chest, he could feel her shivering.

"Dr. Slater!" Eddie called as he came across the doctor collecting his medical supplies. "She has a fever." Eddie carried her to the back of the wagon and met the doctor there. Holding her in his arms, Eddie held her still while Dr. Slater started to check her over.

"Definitely has a fever, and a bad one, too. She's already starting to shake. We need to get her out of these clothes. The layers are probably not helping at all," Dr. Slater said as he hopped onto the wagon and started to clear a space. "We'll get her laid out here once it's comfortable enough."

Sawyer and Gray came walking back to the wagon, leading a robber each ahead of them. Once they reached the wagon, they tied the robbers to a lead rope off the wagon and then came to help Eddie with Miss Fiona. Together, they were able to use their bedding to make a comfortable space in the back of the wagon where Miss Fiona could rest easily as they made their way back to town.

"Since I'm a doctor, Eddie, it's best if I do this next part by myself," Dr. Slater said. "Just stand guard for me."

Eddie nodded as he hopped out of the wagon and stood behind it with the flap drawn closed, while Dr. Slater made Miss Fiona more comfortable. Petticoats were soon tossed out the back of the wagon, followed by her gown. As the gown was tossed aside, Eddie noticed something gold sailing through the air. As he heard it clank to the ground, Eddie moved quickly towards it until it stopped rolling and was still. Eddie bent down and picked up the small gold ring, wondering why Fiona would have such a thing.

"Alright, you can join me again, Eddie," Dr. Slater called. Eddie pocketed the ring and pulled himself back into the wagon as he folded back one of the flaps to let in sunlight. "Now, I'm going to have you start washing her skin with this clean cloth and buckskin of water. She needs to be cooled down, but not suddenly." Eddie looked down at Miss Fiona. She was undressed down to her chamise. A light blanket covered her, but Eddie blushed nonetheless. He'd been with plenty women before, but had never looked upon a woman this exposed without permission.

As Dr. Slater hopped down from the wagon to start patching up the robbers so they could all head back to town, Eddie did what the doctor had instructed. He took the clean cloth and soaked it with water from the buckskin and began to wash Fiona's face, neck, and arms. Her skin felt so hot to the touch that he feared she wouldn't recover. His anger grew towards the robbers as he wished he could just finish them off right here and now. But he forced himself to stick to his task in the hopes of saving Miss Fiona's life.

Eventually everything was set to head out. With the robbers bound and gagged, they were saddled onto their horses and tethered behind the wagon. The goal was to reach the town by nightfall in an effort to find better medical care for Miss Fiona. Eddie allowed Sawyer to drive the wagon as he remained in the back with Miss Fiona, helping to keep her from swaying too much as the wagon was moved forward.

Eddie was so focused on Miss Fiona's face, praying that she would wake up soon, that he paid little attention to what was going on around him. Eddie felt the rocking of the wagon as they started out of the forest, and as he held Miss Fiona's hand in his, he took in her features. Eddie had to admit that Miss Fiona was a beautiful young woman. The photo she had sent him did little justice to her actual beauty. She had golden hair with a hint of redness to it that made her appear fierce. Her face was defined with high cheekbones, and he could tell that she was taller than most women. He smiled, thinking that she would match him well since he was much taller than his brother. As Eddie looked to her luscious lips, he reasoned that he would very much enjoy kissing her.

But as the convoy of horses, ponies, and the wagon made its way out of the forest and back to town, Eddie only hoped that Miss Fiona would recover from this nightmare.

CHAPTER 11

*F*iona was certain that she was dead. She was surrounded by a bright light, a feeling of comfort all around her. She felt warm, but no longer felt the burning heat in her skin. She was lying down, relaxed in a plush cot. She could smell the scent of flowers nearby and reasoned that she was about to open her eyes to Heaven. But when Fiona finally mustered up the strength to open her eyes, she instead found herself in a small room with white walls. A window was nearby and had the shutters were propped open. A light breeze came into the room from the window, bringing with it the scent of flowers.

As Fiona slowly turned her head and looked about the room, she soon spotted a young man sitting in a wicker chair in the corner. His head was slumped down as he slept, but she instantly recognized him. He had been the one that had been carrying her in the forest. She remembered his light brown hair and how beautifully blue his eyes had been. She was certain he was an angel, but now, as she looked at him properly, she wondered who he really was.

He was unlike any man Fiona had seen before. As she looked over his rugged attire, she figured that he could be the image of all the cowboys she'd ever read about in her novels. He wore a western shirt with a tan vest overtop. Jeans covered his legs and boots stuck out of the bottom. Fiona saw the pistol in the holster on his side, as well as rope on the other. She wondered why this man would be armed, and for a second she feared that perhaps this man could in fact be one of the robbers.

Panicked, Fiona tried to sit up quickly, but the moment she did so her head was flooded with pain. She raised her hand to her forehead as she tried to stifle the cry she was about to release. Her breaths came in heavy gasps as she felt a sickness rise up in her.

"Hey, you shouldn't be up. You need to lie down and rest," came a male voice beside her. Fiona opened her eyes slightly and saw those beautiful blue eyes once more. The man had a gentle expression on his face as he came to sit on the edge of the cot. Softly, he used his hand to ease her down onto the cot once more.

"I'm Eddie Murtaugh," the man explained, causing Fiona gasp with surprise.

"Eddie? From Spruce Valley?" Fiona asked. But when she spoke, she began to cough as her throat was very dry. Eddie quickly gathered a cup of water from a nearby table and helped her drink it all.

"Easy now, Miss Fiona. Yes, I am Eddie from Spruce Valley. Once our sheriff received the telegram that you'd been taken hostage, my friends and I set off immediately to come rescue you. I'm just sorry we didn't reach you sooner," Eddie said in a soft voice.

"I don't remember much after I tried to escape. I had become so weak by the time they recaptured me that it was hard to stay conscious," Fiona explained as she rested her head back down on the pillow.

"You're safe now, Miss Fiona. We are back in Medora. You've been asleep for the last three days as you've recovered from a terrible fever," Eddie explained. As Fiona looked up at him with surprise, he only looked at her with kindness.

"What about the robbers?" Fiona asked, fear finding its way into her mind again.

"They were captured and brought to the town's jail. You won't ever have to worry about them again," Eddie explained. Fiona released a long sigh at the relief of knowing that the robbers had been captured.

"And what about my parents? Is my father here yet?" Fiona asked. She desperately wanted to return home as soon as possible.

"Your father has been sent a telegram, but we've heard no word from him yet," Eddie said with a grim expression.

"What do you mean? If I've been resting for three days, certainly he should have replied to the telegram by now?" Fiona asked in disbelief.

"I agree, Miss Fiona. I'm not sure why there has been no word. However, now that you are awake, I'll send another telegram to let your parents know that you are alive and well. But we'll be leaving for Spruce Valley as soon as you are strong enough to travel," Eddie assured.

"Spruce Valley? But I want to return home," Fiona said before she realized she shouldn't have. She instantly saw the pain in Eddie's eyes and regretted saying those words. She had hoped her father would have come for her by now and she could tell Eddie, upon her departure, that she would rather return to Boston than risk being kidnapped again.

"I understand why you would want to return home, Miss Fiona. After what you've been through, any young lady would want to return to what she is familiar with. I'm sure your first experience with the West hasn't been a pleasant one," Eddie said with his eyes averted from hers. Fiona felt guilty for causing him pain after everything he'd done to save her.

"I'm sorry, Eddie. I'm sure that is disappointing for you to hear," Fiona said, her eyes feeling heavy once more.

"Think nothing of it, Miss. We'll get you well before long and you'll at least get to see Spruce Valley before you go home," Eddie said in a cheerful voice. But Fiona had no strength to reply as she drifted off to sleep once more.

EDDIE SIGHED DEEPLY as he rubbed his fingers through his hair. He was relieved to see that Fiona had woken for a short time but felt saddened to hear that she wanted to return home. After everything she'd gone through to escape her home, he couldn't understand why she would want to return. But as Eddie sat on the edge of her cot in the small medical clinic that was in Medora, he could reason that she was frightened still by everything she'd experienced. He couldn't judge her for wanting to return home, but simply hoped that she'd change her mind once she felt better.

After Eddie made sure that she was resting easy, he got up from the cot and made his way out of the room. At the front of the clinic, he let the nurse know that Fiona had been awake for a time and that he was leaving to let his companions know. She thanked him for staying with Fiona since the clinic had become rather full lately. Eddie simply nodded as he left the clinic and went down the road to the local inn.

Dr. Slater and Josh had decided to stay in town for two reasons. One, because Dr. Slater wanted to keep a watch over Fiona as she recovered. And two, because Josh had instantly become famous from coast to coast after the news was telegrammed across the country that he and his deputies had jailed the infamous train robbers. Josh had been invited to dinner with both the sheriff of Medora, as well as its mayor. Josh was a hero now and was being recognized as such. And therefore, it wouldn't have been wise for Josh to stay with the others outside of town where they had made camp until they could all start the journey back to Spruce Valley.

As Eddie walked down the boardwalk towards the inn, he tried to gather his nerves. He was looking forward to letting the others know that Fiona had woken up for a time and that her fever was gone. But his stomach tightened in knots over the fact that she wanted to return home. Eddie felt grim indeed as he entered the inn, and found Dr. Slater and Josh in the dining room where lunch was being served.

"Eddie, it's good to see you," Josh said with a smile. He'd been enjoying the publicity, but once he seemed to recognize

Eddie's face, he quieted down and motioned towards the chair next to him.

"Has something happened to Fiona?" Dr. Slater asked as Eddie sat down.

"Fiona's fever broke in the night and she just woke up. We talked for a few minutes before she fell asleep again. I helped her drink some water, explained that she was safe, and that her kidnappers were in jail," Eddie explained.

"Well, that sounds fantastic. So why do you look so grave, Eddie?" Josh asked.

"She wants to go home. She doesn't understand why her father hasn't come for her, and I explained that we would be traveling to Spruce Valley as soon as she is well enough to travel. I fear that this whole experienced has frightened her so much that she's willing to return to the life she once ran from," Eddie explained grimly.

"I can't blame her, Eddie," Dr. Slater spoke up. "She was in a bad way when we found her, and God only knows what she went through when she was kidnapped. She didn't have any bruising and didn't look to have been forced upon, but there are other ways to torture a lady. She could now be malnourished. She was probably forced to sleep out in the open."

Eddie nodded. He could understand why Fiona would want to return home as quickly as possible. "I get that, Doc. I just wasn't expecting it, is all," Eddie said in a somber voice.

"Well, she'll come home to Spruce Valley, and I'll telegram her father to let him know that she is awake and well and will be coming back with us. I doubt she'll want to stay alone in Medora," Josh reasoned.

"Was the same thing I told her as well," Eddie commented. "Well, I'm going to ride out and go visit with the others. I'm sure she'll be awake by supper time and will be as hungry as a bear after winter."

"I'll go stay with her until you return, Eddie," Dr. Slater said.

"I appreciate it, Doc. I appreciate everything you two have done," Eddie said as he stood.

"Don't you worry one bit, Eddie. Go spend some time with your monkey and brother, and we'll see you after a bit," Josh said. Eddie nodded and smiled at the joke before he left and made his way back to the main street to collect his Indian pony.

As Eddie trotted out of town towards the place where the others had been camping out, Eddie tried to see the bright side of the situation. Fiona had been rescued and she was currently recovering from having a severe fever. Eddie understood that it would take some time to mentally recover from being kidnapped, and he only hoped that Fiona would be able to live the rest of her years in happiness. But the thought of her returning home did something to Eddie that he'd never felt. Having only been with her for a short time, he felt like he would miss her after working so hard to meet her.

Eddie prayed that no matter what happened next, Fiona would finally be able to feel safe again.

IT TOOK another three days in the clinic to feel like she had the strength to travel again. Fiona enjoyed the company while she rested in the small room she'd been assigned. She was able to meet everyone that Eddie had written about in his letters. And she learned for herself just how humorous Dr. Slater and Gray Jenkins could be when they were together. Eddie explained at one point that she would get to meet Bright Star during their journey to Spruce Valley, because they were worried that the locals wouldn't accept the Indian in town. Fiona had to admit that she looked forward to meeting this man and thanking him for everything he'd done to rescue her.

As time went on and Fiona regained her strength, she enjoyed her time alone with Eddie. They talked about all sorts of things but were careful not to mention her time with the robbers. Everyone had been kind enough not to bring up the subject around her. Instead, Eddie described what it would be like to travel to Spruce Valley with the others, that she'd be able to ride up front in the wagon with him, or if she wanted to, she could try her luck with horseback riding.

"I'm not sure if I would be any good at it," Fiona said, though she thought riding a horse might be some fun.

"Well, we all recently had to learn how to ride bareback. I think Bright Star is a good teacher, and we would all make sure you didn't get hurt. I doubt that we'll be traveling at the same pace that we did coming up here," Eddie assured.

The one thing that Fiona was learning about Eddie was that he was a very kind and considerate man. He was not only handsome, but the very sight of him made her smile. As she waited for her body to feel strong enough to travel, she looked forward to talking to him each day. Though, every time he did come to visit with her, she always asked him if he'd heard back from her father.

Fiona was overcome with so many emotions every time Eddie shared the disheartening news with her that still there had been no word from her parents. A part of her wondered if they were currently traveling by train and therefore hadn't received the messages. But when Sheriff Ryder had sent a telegram down the trainline as a sheriff on the lookout for her parents, there had still been no reply. Fiona was starting to think that her parents did not truly care about her and if returning home was the answer anymore.

However, Fiona did her best to put that out of her mind because first she would be traveling to Spruce Valley. From there, she would have to determine her own future. With the extended invitation from Dr. Slater to join him and his family during her stay, Fiona knew that she had much to look forward to. She would be traveling with a group of armed men who would protect her from any danger, and there was much about Spruce Valley that she looked forward to discovering.

On the morning of their departure, Fiona rose from her cot in the medical clinic and put on the traveling gown that the nurse had lent her. She disliked the fact that she owned so few items and had to borrow clothing from other women. But she reasoned that this was the way things were done out West. There weren't women's clothing stores on every corner like she had been used to in Boston.

A knock on the door sounded, and Fiona called to the person to come in as she finished pinning back her hair. Though she often had it curled and pinned for her, Fiona had been taught how to braid her hair by the nurse in order to keep it out of her face. Eddie came into the room carrying a bouquet of wildflowers.

"Good day, Fiona. I picked these for you on my way into town this morning from the camp," Eddie said as he handed Fiona the small bundle. She was surprised and happy as she accepted the flowers and inhaled their sweet aroma.

"Why thank you, Eddie," Fiona said as she held onto them. Fiona looked around the room and realized she had no other things to collect. "I guess I'm ready to be off." Fiona was further surprised when Eddie extended his arm to her in a very gentlemanly fashion. She smiled as she took his arm and allowed him to lead her out of the clinic.

"The others are waiting for us just on the outskirts of town. It shouldn't be a long walk," Eddie explained, as they left the clinic after a quick goodbye to the nurse and resident doctor. Though it was far from the nearest city, Fiona had to admit that the medical care she'd received had been excellent.

"I think a long walk will do me good. I've been cooped up for so long that I shall look forward to any amount of exercise," Fiona replied. She was also enjoying being so close to Eddie as they walked at a leisurely pace.

"When we reach the others, I have a surprise for you as well," Eddie said with a smirk.

Fiona smiled up at him, enjoying his handsome features. "You seem to be full of surprises this morning, Mr. Murtaugh," Fiona said with a chuckle.

"I will admit that I always enjoy impressing a young lady," Eddie replied.

"Then I shall consider myself lucky to be the current young lady in your sights," Fiona said, surprised at how easy it was to flirt with Eddie. She'd never acted this way towards a man before and couldn't reason why she felt so comfortable with it now.

"Miss Fiona, you are the only woman in my sights," Eddie reassured her with a serious tone of voice. Fiona smiled at Eddie with a simple nod of her head. She knew she shouldn't encourage Eddie since she still thought of going back to Boston. Her future was so uncertain that she didn't want to commit to starting a relationship with Eddie when she wasn't even sure how long she'd be in his company.

As they traveled out of town, Fiona quickly spotted a covered wagon in the distance that was surrounded by several horses. But as they drew closer, she realized that they weren't just any horses. They were Indian ponies that were currently being ridden bareback, just as Eddie had described. And on one such horse was a tall Indian man with long black hair with bits of gray weaved through it. He wore a buckskin tunic and leggings, and his feet were dressed in moccasins. Fiona had read about Indians several times before, but never thought she'd ever get to see one, let alone meet one.

As Fiona and Eddie drew closer to the group, they were greeted warmly. "Good day to you, Miss Fiona. It's good to see you out and about on this fine day," Dr. Slater said.

"Thank you, Dr. Slater. I have much thanks to give to you for keeping such a close watch on me," Fiona replied.

"Just don't be thanking him the whole way home. His ego is already this big," Sheriff Ryder said, holding his hands up far from each other.

"This coming from the sheriff that is currently full of himself," piped up Gray.

"Hey! It's not every day that you get to bring in a gang like that," the sheriff retorted. Just the mention of the robbers caused Fiona to stiffen.

"Well, let's get ready to move out. First, Bright Star. May I introduce you officially to Miss Fiona Wilkins," Eddie spoke up. Fiona was thankful that Eddie had changed the subject so quickly. He then led Fiona over to where the Indian was positioned upon the pony. And as Fiona drew closer, she realized that a monkey sat on his shoulders.

"It is nice to meet you, Fiona Wilkins. I am proud to have accompanied these fine men to rescue you," Bright Star said in greeting.

"Thank you very much, Bright Star, for all that you've done. I hope one day I will be able to repay you," Fiona said. And though she didn't mean to be rude, she couldn't help staring at the monkey that seemed to be staring back at her as well.

Eddie made a clicking noise next to her and as Fiona turned her head to see what he was doing, a moment later the monkey was scurrying down from Bright Star's shoulder, finding a new position on Eddie's shoulders. Fiona was so surprised that she stepped away from Eddie quickly as she and the monkey came face to face.

"Don't worry, there's nothing to be afraid of," Eddie reassured her as she stared wide eyed at the monkey.

"Forgive me, Mr. Murtaugh. The monkey is just surprising, is all," Fiona said, regaining her composure. After taking a deep breath, Fiona stepped forward and reached out her hand towards the monkey. It made cute sounds as Fiona petted the monkey's fur, which she found surprisingly soft.

"His name is Jack, and it takes everyone a few minutes to get used to him," Eddie said reassuringly.

"Except me, of course," Bright Star said with a laugh.

"Yes, Bright Star. Jack has taken quite a liking to you," Eddie said as he looked towards the Indian.

"Alrighty folks, let's get a move on. Home is not close by," Sheriff Ryder spoke up. Eddie then escorted Fiona over to the wagon and pulled back the cover to reveal the inside. As Fiona's eyes fell upon her suitcases, she could hardly believe her eyes.

"How did you ever retrieve them?" Fiona asked in disbelief.

"While you were resting, I inquired with the train depot. The suitcases were amongst others in the lost and found with your name on the handles. They were easy enough to locate, and I kept them in the wagon 'til you were recovered," Eddie explained. "You'll be able to ride comfortable back here. There's plenty of blankets to sit on and you'll be able to lay down if you need to."

Fiona was still shocked as Eddie helped her up into the wagon. He showed her the best place to position her foot and she climbed onto the wagon with ease. She was surrounded by supplies as she got into the wagon, but she found the pile of blankets Eddie had pointed out and sat upon them to get as comfortable as she could. A moment later, Eddie was rounding the wagon and pulling himself up onto the driver's seat before slapping the reins to get the horses moving.

It took a second for Fiona to get used to the movements of the wagon. It was much like riding on the train, but much more jarring every time one of the wheels would hit a rock or bump in the road. Fiona reminded herself that a little bump here and there was better than what she had to endure a few days ago. It wasn't the most comfortable way to travel, but Fiona was simply glad to be traveling.

As they traveled along the main road, the sun continued to rise in the sky. Fiona took the time to open her suitcases and look over the contents to see if most of her things were still intact. She was pleased to discover that all her things had been left alone in the suitcase, including her traveling gowns and personal things. She found her novel and placed it in her lap before closing the suitcases back up, pushing them to the side. Even though she'd read the novel a dozen times before, she felt excited to read it again, simply because she had the freedom to do so.

Fiona was very thankful for having been rescued, and as she continued to sneak glances at Eddie from over the top of her book, she was especially grateful to have met him in the process.

CHAPTER 12

Traveling to Spruce Valley had several ups and downs for Fiona. She enjoyed the company during their days of travel, getting to laugh and joke with many of them. Fiona was made to feel at ease and comfortable in the way she was respected, since she was the only female traveling in the group. She was certainly enjoying the scenery as the wagon rolled along the road, delivering sights of hills, forests, and open plains.

But at night, the nightmares would come again and again. Tucked safely in the wagon with several layers of bedding and blankets, Fiona would toss and turn in her nightgown. Images of pain and fear would rush through her head as she tried to fight off invisible assailants. And when she would wake with a start, she'd quickly sit up and take several seconds to realize that she was safe in the covered wagon. Fiona would have to sit still for a while, listening to the sounds of the night. She'd look towards the front of the wagon and out into the open sky to see stars shining. It would be a while before she tried to sleep again, but she took some comfort in knowing that she was surrounded by several brave men. Even if some of them snored loudly at night.

One morning, Eddie invited her to ride up front on the bench of the wagon. "But what about Sawyer?" Fiona had asked.

"I didn't get much sleep last night and wouldn't mind stretching my legs out back there," Sawyer spoke up in his defense.

"Well, alright then," Fiona agreed, standing steadily to her feet as the wagon rumbled down the road. She'd gotten used to the feeling of the wagon's movements and took small steps in order to switch places with Sawyer. Once she neared the bench, he hopped into the back of the wagon as though it was standing still, and then helped her up onto the bench.

"Thank you, Sawyer," Fiona said with a sigh of relief when she was safely sitting on the bench. Sawyer nodded in return as he made his way towards the back of the wagon and started fashioning himself a comfortable spot to lay down on.

"Seems like Sawyer isn't the only one whose been having trouble at night," Eddie spoke up as he moved closer to her. His eyes stayed on the horses and the road ahead, but he seemed attentive to her as well.

Fiona sighed as she looked out into the distance, enjoying the scenery as the morning sun made its progression through the sky. "Is it that obvious?" Fiona asked, worried that her nightmares had woken someone else.

"We heard your frightened cries last night," Eddie stated. "I did rise to check on you, only to see you were dreaming.

Bright Star wants to do a cleansing ceremony on you tonight, if you'd be willing?"

Fiona looked at Eddie then, a feeling of both embarrassment and curiosity came over her. "What does this ceremony entail?" she asked.

"The way Bright Star explained it is that you'll get to sit comfortably while he prays over you," Eddie explained.

Fiona thought about it and reasoned that it didn't sound terrifying. "I could use all the prayers I could get," Fiona reasoned. Eddie smiled and nodded his head.

"I always enjoy seeing Indian ceremonies, so I think you'll enjoy it," Eddie reassured. "Dr. Slater suggested that you could use some laudanum to help you sleep."

"I would rather not use anything that I could get addicted to. I've seen businessmen blackmail doctors into giving them more," Fiona said.

"I'm sure Dr. Slater wouldn't let something like that happen, but I respect your reasonings. I simply don't want you to suffer any more than you already have," Eddie said. Eddie's words surprised Fiona. She looked to him and watched him for a long moment. A smile crept onto his face as he turned his eyes to her.

"Why you lookin' at me like that?" he asked.

Fiona blushed as she realized she was staring. She looked away as she said, "Because I'm surprised by your gentleman-like characteristics. I never thought a cowboy could possess such kindness as you've shown me," Fiona said, her head lowered. She was further surprised when she felt Eddie's hand gently tilt her head towards him.

"You deserve all the kindness in the world, Fiona, after

what you experienced in North Dakota, but also back in Boston. No one should ever have to experience what you've gone through, and I hope that spending time in Spruce Valley will be a comfort to you," Eddie explained as their eyes locked. Fiona was so lost in his gaze and touched by his words that she was hardly aware of herself as she leaned towards him.

However, Eddie broke their eye contact as he quickly looked back to the horses and moved them to the left to keep the wagon on the road. Him breaking their eye contact was like being pulled from a magical spell. Fiona took several deep breaths as she realized she was about to kiss Eddie. She had no idea where these deep feelings had come from. She reasoned that she was simply recovering from being kidnapped and any amount of kindness felt almost surreal to her.

Having regained control of her emotions, Fiona knew she had to be more careful around Eddie. After all, she still planned to return to Boston.

EDDIE HAD ENJOYED SPENDING the day talking with Fiona. Getting to make her laugh seemed worth all the effort since her laugh often sounded like music to him. Every once and a while, Jack would come over to him from where he enjoyed riding with Bright Star. During those times, Fiona spent time petting Jack's fur and feeding him dates. Eventually, Jack moved over to Fiona's shoulder and she would giggle and talk sweetly to the monkey.

Sometimes, Eddie liked to think that Fiona was coming to

Spruce Valley to be with him. She was not only beautiful, but had a sweet spirit that Eddie found lovely. He didn't like to think that she'd be gone from his life when her parents arrived to take her home. Eddie wasn't certain that they would ever come since there had been no word from them, but he knew that returning to Boston was Fiona's current plan for the future.

That night, as they made camp off from the road, they sat around the fire to enjoy one of Gray's cooked meals. For being a Boston socialite, Fiona had adapted well to traveling on the open road. She hadn't complained about having to sleep in a wagon or eat rustic food, since ingredients were few. She easily talked with everyone and could guess that her experience in social settings afforded her the ease of speaking. And Eddie felt proud when she even included Bright Star in the conversation.

As the meal came to an end, and Sawyer and Josh went off to take care of washing the dishes in a nearby stream, Eddie was sitting next to Fiona talking about cattle drives when Bright Star approached them. He kneeled in front of Fiona, which seemed to surprise her a moment.

"Fiona Wilkins, I would like to perform a cleansing ceremony on you now. I believe it will help settle your spirit so that you may move forward and away from the darkness of your past," Bright Star explained. Eddie watched Fiona's expression as she looked at the Indian. She looked nervous, but eventually she nodded her head with a small smile.

Bright Star smiled in return as he rose once more and tossed a satchel into the fire. A pleasing smell of herbs filled the air as Bright Star started to chant and sing. He removed a large feather from his hair and started to fan the smoke from the fire around Fiona. He began to stomp his feet to the rhythm of the song he was chanting.

Everyone watched with respect and interest as Bright Star performed the ceremony. It was as though nothing else in the world mattered, as they listened to his chanting and watched the way he danced and fanned the smoke from the fire. As Eddie shifted his eyes to Fiona, he saw how intently she was watching Bright Star too, with tears in her eyes.

In that moment, Eddie wanted to do everything in his power to take all the fear away from her. He wanted to protect her with his very life and ensure that she never felt this type of pain again. Eddie mindlessly stroked Jack's fur as he watched the performance with the monkey sat on his shoulder, thinking that he needed to do something to convince Fiona to stay in Spruce Valley and give their relationship an honest chance.

As Bright Star's ceremony came to an end, the night seemed to fill with a deafening silence. Sawyer and Josh had returned from their chores and had stood on the outside of their circle as they watched and listened. It was Fiona's voice that eventually broke the trance they had all been in.

"Thank you, Bright Star. You have a wonderful voice and you dance very well," Fiona said.

Bright Star smiled keenly in return as he nodded his head. "You shall make a great wife one day, Fiona Wilkins. If you are ever in need of a husband, I have two sons who would be honored to have you as a wife," Bright Star said. His words startled Eddie, thinking that Bright Star was offering one of his sons to Fiona. As she laughed, he wondered what was so funny.

"Thank you, Bright Star, but I am not in need of a husband at this moment. And I would not consider a man whom I have not yet met," Fiona replied, her mirth subsiding.

"Well then. We shall come visit you at the Slater's Ranch during our visit to Spruce Valley, and perhaps then we could convince you otherwise," Bright Star said with a wink, replacing the large black feather into his hair once more. Then, he took a seat around the fire next to Dr. Slater as the two struck up a conversation.

"How did you enjoy the ceremony?" Eddie asked as he drew Fiona's attention back to him. Fiona reached out and petted Jack as she gathered her thoughts.

"It was like being hypnotized," Fiona said. "It was wonderful to see and filled me with a lot of peace. I have never been prayed over like that before and I am grateful to have had the experience."

Eddie smiled at her, thinking she had the perfect response. He had felt the same too, and wondered if the others had felt it.

"I was certainly not expecting Bright Star's offer," Fiona said in a soft voice, as she began to giggle once more. Eddie joined her as he nodded his head.

"He did the same thing to Gray's wife when she first came to Spruce Valley. It seems that Bright Star is constantly on the lookout for a decent wife for his sons. The Crow Tribe has a small camp on the outskirts of Spruce Valley. There is a small number of them now compared to what they used to be. Soon, they'll travel south for the winter to follow the buffalo herd," Eddie explained.

"It will be sad to see him go," Fiona said softly as she

turned her eyes back to the fire. Eddie wasn't sure what to say in response. A part of him wondered if she had considered staying for an extended period in Spruce Valley. He certainly hoped so..

THE NEXT MORNING brought a wave of excitement for Fiona. Not only had she slept soundly for the first time in what felt like weeks, but this would be the day that they finally arrived in Spruce Valley and the Slater Ranch. Fiona was looking forward to being surrounded by four walls again instead of out in the open. She'd enjoyed the nice weather and getting to see the stars as she laid down, but the thought of sleeping in a real bed since she ran away from Boston was something she was desperately looking forward to.

Fiona had been back and forth with her thoughts over what she would do for her future. A part of her desperately wanted to return to Boston, hoping to please her parents enough to allow her to marry someone she at least liked. And the other part of her −the part that was healing more rapidly with every passing day −wanted to rediscover her courage and strength once more in order to make her way in the West. Either way, she was excited to meet Mrs. Slater and Mrs. Jenkins, since they'd both been mail-order-brides from the East.

Fiona was sitting up front with Eddie once more, having passed up her opportunity to ride one of the Indian ponies. She felt like she wasn't quite ready to start riding yet, but Eddie had started to show her how to lead the wagon. With the reins in her hands, and Eddie sitting very close to her, he instructed her on how tight to hold them, how to steer the horses, and how to tell them to pick up their pace.

"Relax your arms," Eddie guided. "You don't want to go stiff and lose strength in your arms." Fiona smiled as she tried to relax. She'd never done anything like this before and found steering the four large horses to be thrilling. It was an easy enough task, but Fiona feared doing something wrong.

"When we get home, I can show you how to unhook the horses from the wagon so that you can learn for yourself how it's done. So, if you ever need to ride into town, you can at least take the wagon," Eddie offered.

"It seems I'll have to learn a lot once we reach the ranch," Fiona reasoned as she kept her eyes to the road ahead of them.

"Yes. But you won't be alone. You'll have Mrs. Slater and Mrs. Jenkins, who will be eager teachers. I'm confident that if I can learn to read and write from the Slaters, then you can learn a few things about living in the West from them as well," Eddie said with confidence.

Fiona was certainly appreciating his tone of voice. He always seemed to be so positive, and though Fiona had many fears about her immediate future, she took comfort in knowing she would be close to Eddie through it all.

The sun was high in the sky when the first sights of the Slater Ranch came into view. Fiona craned her neck this way and that to see everything she could. A small one-story, white clapboard ranch house stood in the distance. A large red barn had been erected farther away with wooden fencing running out from the back of it. Several horses grazed in the pasture and she could make out the shape of cattle in the distance. The sight made her feel excited to be seeing a real Western home.

She couldn't believe that she was finally arriving at their destination at long last, and the thought of not having to travel any longer brought tears of relief to Fiona's eyes.

A sea of prairie grass stretched out as far as Fiona could see, meeting the dazzling blue sky above the horizon. Maple and birch trees dotted the ranch and there was a white bunkhouse on the right of the driveway that seemed to stretch on forever. Fiona assumed that Eddie stayed in the bunkhouse with the other cattle hands and seeing how close it was to the main house, she knew that she'd be able to see Eddie plenty.

"Home sweet home," Dr. Slater said as he urged his pony forward. Gray was right on his heels as they seemed to race each other towards the house. Fiona chuckled as she watched them race across the prairie, practically leaping off their ponies before dashing inside the house where a choir of happy voices sounded.

"Well fellas, it's been a real pleasure. Fiona, welcome to Spruce Valley," Josh said as he tipped his hat towards her and then made his way towards the barn.

"It is good to be back," Sawyer spoke up from the back of the wagon.

"Yeah, I would agree with that. It's been fun traveling, but nothing quite beats home," Eddie replied.

"I will need to take the ponies back to camp and prepare for our journey south," Bright Star spoke up. Eddie pulled the wagon to a stop in front of the ranch house.

"Thank you again, Bright Star, for helping us when you are so close to leaving Spruce Valley. I shall think of something to bring you when you return," Eddie spoke up.

"Perhaps Jack would like to accompany me south for the

winter?" Bright Star asked. "That way he will not have to worry about the fierce cold weather."

Fiona noticed the surprised look on Eddie's face as he looked towards the Indian. He even held Jack close to him as he regarded the other man.

"I will have to think about that, Bright Star. You make a valid point, but I am very fond of Jack and would surely miss him," Eddie replied. Bright Star only nodded his head and grunted as he led his pony in the direction of the barn. Fiona sat with Eddie for a moment before the ranch house doors swung open and two ladies came strolling out.

"Welcome, welcome!" called the one with long black hair. She had dazzling green eyes that Fiona found lovely. She also realized that this woman was dressed in the sophisticated manner with which Fiona was used to back in Boston.

"My name is Mrs. Lucy Slater. And this is my business partner, Mrs. Martha Jenkins," the black-haired woman introduced. Eddie quickly hopped down from the wagon and came around to help Fiona down as well.

"Mrs. Slater, Mrs. Jenkins. It's a pleasure to meet you both. My name is Miss Fiona Wilkins, from Boston," Fiona said as she dipped her head towards the two married women.

"Fiona, we are so glad to finally meet you. Eddie has told us so many wonderful things about you from your letters that I feel like we know you already," Mrs. Jenkins spoke up. She had lovely red hair and bright blue eyes that shone with kindness.

"I will admit that Eddie spoke highly of both of you as well. I am pleased to finally get to meet you," Fiona replied.

"And we are so glad the whole business is behind ye. It

seems that mail-order-brides can't seem to catch a break when coming to Spruce Valley," Mrs. Slater commented. "When I first came here, there were these nasty men harassing us because they wanted the ranch."

"And I certainly brought trouble with me," Mrs. Jenkins added.

"Does Spruce Valley get much crime?" Fiona asked, frightened at the idea of having to deal with robbers again.

"No, dear. It was all very circumstantial. My goodness, we are probably frightening you. Come on in and let's get you settled. The little ones are eager to meet you and there is a water closet you can use to bathe and whatnot," Mrs. Jenkins said as she came to Fiona and took her hand, leading her up the front porch stairs.

"I'll bring your stuff inside in a bit," Eddie called after her. Fiona turned and waved at him, giving him a smile before she was led inside the ranch house.

Fiona hadn't expected the ranch house to look so modern. There were several elements that reminded her of her home in Boston. There was a formal dining room, sitting room, and in the back was the kitchen. A large stove rested in a spacious kitchen. Fiona was even surprised to see an icebox.

As Fiona was taking in all the finery, she saw Dr. Slater and Gray in the sitting room, playing with two children on the floor like two overgrown children themselves. One girl, who was slightly older than the boy, ramped on the two gentlemen, climbing on their backs and riding them like horses as the men crawled around on the floor. Fiona couldn't help but laugh at the sight since she knew both these men to be quite serious at times.

"Ye'd never think that Sam and Gray would act like this with the children," Mrs. Slater said with a shake of her head.

"Well, I'm sure they've missed them," Mrs. Jenkins said as she continued to lead Fiona through the house. She was led down a hallway and shown the water closet, then the spare bedroom. "I stayed in this room when I first came to Spruce Valley as well," Mrs. Jenkins said as Fiona walked around the room. It was stylishly decorated with a large bed that looked very inviting. There was a dresser and a writing desk in the room with beautiful curtains that hung over the window. As Fiona peeked through, she could see plenty of people coming and going. She even spotted Eddie in the distance.

"This is a very lovely room," Fiona said as she turned back to the two women. "I am very thankful, Mrs. Slater, for your hospitality. I've very much looked forward to arriving and not having to be out on the open road any longer."

"Please Miss Fiona, simply call me Lucy. We are both big city girls, but things are much less formal here," Mrs. Slater replied.

"Yes, and simply call me Martha. I like to think we'll make quick friends," Mrs. Jenkins added. Fiona simply smiled because she didn't want to be rude in stating that she didn't plan to stay in Spruce Valley longer than when her parents would surely come to get her. Her inner turmoil was still raging over what she should do about her future. But for now, she was simply thankful to be out of a wagon and surrounded by four walls once more.

Just then, Eddie came walking into the room with her two suitcases. He set them down easily at the foot of the bed like they weighed nothing. He certainly continued to surprise

Fiona with his skills, and for a moment she couldn't help but wonder what it might feel like to be wrapped up in those strong arms. Pulling her eyes away from Eddie, she smiled pleasantly at the two women who seemed to be watching her keenly.

"Thank you, Eddie. I appreciate your help," Fiona spoke up, before she completely lost all sense of manners.

"Of course, Fiona. I'm glad to help. But I'll be off for a while. There is much unpacking to do, and I told Bright Star I'd help him return the ponies to his tribe for everything he's done for us," Eddie explained. "I left Jack with Sawyer if you need a friend." He winked at her before leaving the room. Fiona couldn't refrain from blushing as she watched him leave the room.

"Well, we'll let ye get settled," Lucy said with a smile. "Take your time, and feel free to use the water closet across the hallway."

"We'll go put on some hot water so you can take a bath. I know that's what I always wanted after being out on the road for days," Martha spoke up. The two ladies then left the room, Martha closing the door behind her.

It had been so long since Fiona had been by herself that it almost felt strange. There had been a time when she'd enjoyed spending hours alone in her room. But as she stood and looked around the quaint space, she couldn't help but feel an immediate sense of loneliness. She didn't like the feeling at all and quickly went to work on putting her things away in the dresser before selecting a nice dress and under garments to change into. Her nice house slippers had been ruined, so all she had was one set of traveling boots. Fiona reasoned it would have to do for now.

Taking her things to the water closet, Fiona was pleasantly surprised by the space of the room. A large cast iron tub was fashioned into the room, along with the flushing commode. It reminded her much of home, and Fiona was once again thankful that the Slaters had offered to house her. With no money to her name, Fiona wasn't certain how long she would be able to survive on her own in the West.

After taking care of her business and hanging up her nice clothes, Fiona opened the door and ventured back into the kitchen with the intention of helping with heating the hot water. In Boston, the water in her house had been heated by a central boiler and then piped to the water closet. But from the novels Fiona had read, she understood that things were done differently in the West when boilers weren't a common thing to have.

"I hope ye've found everything to yer liking," Lucy said as Fiona came into the kitchen.

"Yes, very much. I am pleasantly surprised that a Western home has a water closet," Fiona admitted.

Lucy chuckled as she lifted a lid on a large pot and checked to see if the water was bubbling yet as wood burned from within the stove. As she replaced the lid, she fully turned to Fiona. "When I came to Spruce Valley almost two years ago, there was much about this ranch house that surprised me. Sam certainly spoils me," Lucy said.

Two children came toddling into the kitchen then as Martha led them by the hands. "The men are going to go get things settled. Seems they'll be busy 'til dinner time," Martha explained. "But in the meantime, we shall certainly have a nice visit. Fiona, may I introduce you to Francene Slater and Samuel Jenkins."

Fiona smiled at the children as she bent down to greet them. "It's a pleasure to meet you," Fiona said as she waved at the children. Francene seemed a bit shy, but Samuel was quick to break from his mother's grasp and wrap his little arms around Fiona. She laughed as she picked up the boy and rested him on her hip.

"Why hello there," Fiona said as the two chuckled together. Samuel then grabbed onto Fiona's braided hair and began playing with it.

"Oh, Samuel likes to play with hair, unfortunately," Martha said as she came to retrieve her son.

"Don't worry, Martha. I'm not worried about my hair at this point. He could not do any more harm to it than the open road has," Fiona said as she handed Samuel to Martha.

"Well, the water seems to be ready. Help me carry it to the tub and ye'll be all set to have a nice, long bath," Lucy spoke up. Fiona was quick to help the woman lift the large pot from the stove using several hand towels. Together, they carefully carried it down the hallway to the water closet while Martha kept a close eye on the kids. Once the hot water had been poured into the tub, Lucy was able to carry it once more by herself.

"There ye go, my dear. Feel free to use whatever ye find in the cupboard," Lucy said before heading back down the hallway.

As Fiona closed the door, she released a long sigh. She was so excited to take a bath that she quickly discarded her clothes right onto the floor and stepped into the tub. She exhaled deeply as she lowered herself into the water. With a bar of soap she'd found in the cupboard, Fiona planned to scrub every inch of her body thoroughly. It wasn't just the grime of traveling for days that was bugging Fiona, she also wanted to rid herself of every bad thing that had happened to her since she left Boston.

Tears stung her eyes as she lathered up the soap and began to wash her body. She eventually unbraided her hair and plunged her head underwater. The hot water did wonders for her skin and hair but no matter what she did, she couldn't seem to stop the tears from sliding down her cheeks. Fiona clasped a hand over her mouth as the sobs came. The last thing she wanted to do was alert someone to the pain that was coursing through her body. She tried to focus on washing her hair instead of the memories that seemed to flash through her mind.

It was a long while before Fiona was able to get in control of her emotions once more. The water had started to turn cold as Fiona finally got out of the tub, pulled the plug at the bottom, and dried herself off with a towel. She felt better than she had in days and was thankful for the opportunity to bathe. After dressing once more, Fiona used her comb to brush her long hair, and when she was done, she decided to simply tie back the top part to keep her hair out of her face. She reckoned that if this town was less formal, she could visit with others with her hair down.

After taking her soiled clothing back to her room and storing them in her suitcase until she could find the time to properly wash them, Fiona then made her way back down the hallway to the main part of the house. There, she found Martha and Lucy busy in the kitchen while the two toddlers sat on the floor playing with wooden blocks. Fiona was amused as she watched the children stack blocks on top of each other, as though they were competing with who could build the tallest tower.

"I bet you are feeling better," Martha spoke up, drawing Fiona's attention to her. Fiona smiled as she nodded her head.

"It's amazing what a simple bath can do to help wash away days of road grime," Fiona said.

"I hope yer hungry, Fiona. We plan to cook a feast in honor of yer arrival," Lucy said happily.

"Oh, I don't want you two going to any trouble," Fiona said quickly, surprised by the generosity.

"Nonsense. I'm sure everyone is starving from Gray's simple cooking," Lucy replied.

Fiona chuckled. "He's not a bad cook with what he had to work with. I've certainly eaten worse," Fiona said, remembering the food she was forced to eat while she'd been kidnapped. The very thought seemed to settle Fiona into remaining quiet.

"Well then, why don't you give us a hand? I'm sure we could teach you a thing or two about cooking," Martha suggested. Fiona focused on the woman and mustered up a smile.

"I've been taught to cook a few dishes, so I'm certain I could be of good help," Fiona said proudly.

"That is a blessing to hear, for sure. When I first came to Spruce Valley, I'd never cooked for meself before. Yer already more well off than I was when first becoming a mail-order-bride," Lucy said happily. Fiona couldn't help but smile at the woman's words. She knew it was better to keep a happy expression on her face instead of telling them that she didn't know if she'd stay in Spruce Valley for long.

As Fiona worked alongside the two women, she quickly realized how lovely it was to be around them. Fiona had missed female companionship and thought that Martha and Lucy would make wonderful friends. As they worked together to prepare dinner, Fiona also looked forward to visiting with Eddie once more.

CHAPTER 13

By the time dinner was ready up at the ranch house, Eddie was certainly looking forward to sitting down and enjoying a home-cooked meal. It felt like weeks since he'd had a proper meal, and though he had to credit Gray for being able to put together some good meals, he couldn't deny that he looked forward to some of Mrs. Slater's home-cooking.

Eddie was also looking forward to getting to spend some more time with Fiona. They'd had plenty of opportunities to talk over the last few days since traveling from North Dakota, but he knew that things would be different now that they could both settle down. Eddie would be returning to work tomorrow, and Fiona would no doubt begin to find her own way in Spruce Valley. He only hoped that she would decide to make this place her home instead of a temporary place to be.

After helping Bright Star take all his ponies to camp, Eddie bathed thoroughly, using a new bar of soap, in the stream that ran along the eastern part of the ranch. He was hoping to make a good impression on Fiona once she saw him all cleaned up. He even took the time to shave and dress in his best clothes. At least, the clothes that were the cleanest. After traveling for countless days, Eddie didn't have too many pairs of clean pants and still hoped to show Fiona that he could clean up well.

"Somethin' sure smells better," Sawyer joked, as Eddie came into the bunkhouse to drop off his road clothes. Sawyer was sitting at the main table with Jack in front of him, feeding the monkey dates.

"You should try bathing some time. You'd be surprised how much better you could smell, too," Eddie said with a chuckle as he ducked into his room, deposited his clothes beside his bed, and then walked back out to the main room.

"I think me and the monkey are going to head down to the stream in a moment," Sawyer replied.

"Well, you two better hurry. I'm guessing dinner will be done shortly," Eddie said as he made his way towards the door.

"You're just in a hurry to go see a certain young lady," Sawyer said with a chuckle. Eddie stopped walking for a moment to face his brother.

"I won't deny that I am looking forward to seeing Fiona. I know we've spent all this time together, but I can't help but think that things will be different now that we're not out on the open road," Eddie admitted.

Sawyer nodded his head as he stood and stretched. Jack quickly scooped up his date and climbed on top of Sawyer's shoulder for a personal ride.

"You're probably right, Eddie. She's been through hell and is finally getting to be in one place for more than a day. It might take some time, but I'm sure Fiona will come around to you," Sawyer said, trying to be reassuring.

"I sure hope so. She's talked about returning to Boston after everything she's been through," Eddie confessed with a deep sigh. Sawyer seemed shocked to hear this.

"I can't believe she'd go back after what her parents put her through. You told me how she was practically being sold off to be married to a man twice her age," Sawyer said with heat in his words. Eddie could tell that the news was rallying him up.

"I think she's just scared, Sawyer. So scared that she isn't thinking clearly. All she knows is that she was safe in Boston," Eddie tried to explain.

"The way she described her life in Boston, it didn't sound like she was safe there, either," Sawyer said as he pushed past Eddie and out of the bunkhouse. Eddie took a few minutes to collect himself. Though he knew his brother was the quieter of the two of them, Sawyer didn't shy away from speaking the truth to someone when he felt they needed to hear it. Eddie only hoped that Sawyer would keep his thoughts to himself while Fiona took time to make the decision for herself.

Eddie then made his way from the bunkhouse towards the main house. The sun was starting to set, and Eddie was certainly looking forward to a good meal and a restful night. Though his bed wasn't anything fancy, it would surely feel better than sleeping on the ground with nothing but a bed roll. As Eddie walked up the front porch steps, he could hear happy chatter coming from inside the house. He couldn't help but smirk as he opened the front door and stepped in.

Eddie shut the door behind him as he came into the house. Heavenly smells filled the air as he made his way into the dining room. Gray and Dr. Slater were already seated at the table with their kids on their laps. Fiona had just set a plate on the table, and Eddie's stomach grumbled at the sight of mashed potatoes and gravy. But what really caught his eye was Fiona's good looks. She looked radiant in her pale blue gown, her hair pulled back from her face —he was definitely attracted to her tall, slim frame. But more than that, he simply enjoyed being around her.

"Good evening, Eddie," Fiona said as she came closer to him.

"Hi there, Fiona. You are sure looking fine this evening," Eddie said as he gave her his best smile. He noticed the blush that quickly spread across her checks, and he felt a deep desire to kiss her. But knowing that she was still uncertain about returning to Boston or staying in Spruce Valley, he knew to keep his hands to himself.

"Thank you, Eddie. You look practically transformed," Fiona said with a light chuckle.

"It's amazing what a bath and a shave can do for a man," Eddie said, joining in with her laughter.

"Hello, Eddie. Good to see you back," Martha said as she came carrying another plate of food from the kitchen.

"Good to see you, too, Mrs. Jenkins," Eddie said, his stomach starting to grumble again as Mrs. Slater then came by carrying a large platter of roasted turkey. "My goodness, that all looks amazing."

Fiona laughed, her hand coming up to cover her mouth as she did so. "Well, you best go save your seat at the table. There is more where that came from," she explained before following the ladies back into the kitchen.

"I heard that Miss Fiona helped prepare the meal," Dr. Slater said as Eddie came to sit next to him near the head of the table.

"I believe it. Fiona explained how she'd learned to cook a few things from her housekeeper," Eddie said, as he remembered some of what Fiona had written about.

"A woman who knows how to cook is an important quality in a wife," Gray added as he bounced Samuel on his knee, causing the young boy to cry out with laughter.

Eddie only nodded his head, not wanting to talk about marriage right now. There was so much uncertainty surrounding Fiona right now that he didn't want to get his hopes up. He'd have to be patient and see where things went after today.

As the others gathered for dinner, with Sawyer and Tom joining them from the bunkhouse, everyone settled around the table. Dr. Slater said grace for the meal, giving thanks for their safe return. Then, everyone filled their plates as stories started to be shared about what had been happening around the ranch and Spruce Valley while they'd been gone.

"I about had a heart attack when the paper arrived with the news of Sheriff Ryder. Is it true that you guys all helped to bring in those train robbers?" Tom spoke up as they ate. With Fiona having sat next to Eddie on the bench at the table, he noticed when she went still at the mention of the robbers.

"It is true, Tom, but let's not talk about that here at the

table," Eddie quickly spoke up before anyone else could. He said this in such a stern voice that he hoped that everyone caught his message.

"It's been rather busy at the boutique since you've all been gone. Everyone's been coming in to find out when you all would be home again. Even the men have come in hoping to hear of something," Martha spoke up.. "I never thought we'd ever get men at the shop!"

"I couldn't stop laughing after Mr. Frost left the boutique. Ye should have seen how large his eyes became when he noticed the lady's undergarments," Lucy said with a chuckle.

"Fiona, you should come into town with Lucy and I tomorrow. With the men all returned, we'll have time to show you around," Martha offered.

Eddie was thankful for the turn in the conversation and watched Fiona as he waited to hear her reply. She smiled as she nodded her head. "I would love to see the town. Eddie has written so much about it that I think I'd enjoy putting faces to the many names," Fiona replied. Eddie was relieved to see her so eager and excited. He certainly didn't want her to be fearful anymore.

By the time all the food had been happily eaten and many compliments had been given to the women for a job well done, everyone was quick to retire for the night. The Jenkins' headed to their own home the moment the dining table was cleared. Tom and Sawyer volunteered to wash the dishes so that Dr. Slater and Mrs. Slater could put their daughter to bed together. It gave Eddie the chance to invite Fiona out onto the front porch so they could have a private moment together.

"I feel as though I could sleep the week away," Fiona

commented as they stepped out onto the front porch together. Eddie pulled the front door closed behind him before joining Fiona on the steps. She looked up at the sky, the night clear and the stars bright.

"I feel the same way. But there is much work to get caught up on. Morning will certainly come too soon," Eddie said as he looked up at the stars with her.

"A part of me feels guilty for bringing you all away from your work and families," Fiona said as she kept her eyes to the stars. Eddie looked down at her and, feeling brave, reached out with his hand and titled her head towards him so he could look into her beautiful blue eyes.

"Never, ever feel guilty about what happened, Fiona. We were all very willing to come to your rescue. The moment we got word, we left Spruce Valley immediately. Don't ever feel bad about what happened because it wasn't your fault in the least," Eddie said as they gazed into each other's eyes. Even with the darkness of night, Eddie could see the tears that were collecting in Fiona's eyes. He moved his hand so he could draw Fiona to him, wrapping his arms around her, holding her close.

Eddie ran his hands through Fiona's hair as she began to cry against his chest. Her hands rested on his chest as her shoulders shook as she let out all the pain she'd been holding in. Eddie was willing to stay with her for as long as it took for Fiona to feel calm and safe again. He was enjoying holding her in his arms and wished to do so for the rest of his life. And even though Fiona was indifferent about staying in Spruce Valley, he was glad to have this moment alone with her.

After a while, Fiona leaned back from him, allowing them

to look at each other once more. Eddie smiled down at her, resisting the eager to kiss her.

"I'm so sorry for crying all of a sudden. It's just, I've felt lost in this deep inner turmoil and I simply couldn't help myself when you talked about your willingness to come rescue me. My own parents have done little to right the wrong that was placed against me that it's hard to believe that complete strangers would do such a thing for me," Fiona said, her hands still resting on his chest as he held her close to him.

"I hope that, if anything, you can see that there are real, kind people here in Spruce Valley who are eager to not only be your friends, but help you create a life for yourself," Eddie said, his hope rising once more that perhaps Fiona would decide to stay.

Fiona smiled up at him as she nodded her head. "I can already tell that Lucy and Martha are wonderful women, and so brave for raising two little children while managing a business. It's such an unheard thing that they really do inspire me," Fiona admitted.

Eddie could not deny that the two married women were very courageous. "I think Western women have more freedoms to create their own future. Society here isn't quick to judge because we are all doing our best to survive and make a life for ourselves," Eddie said. "I know this could be a good place for you to create whatever life you wanted."

As Eddie looked down at Fiona, he silently pleaded that she would reconsider ever returning to Boston. But as Fiona pushed away from Eddie, forcing his arms to fall once more to his sides, he felt a yearning to feel her in his arms once more.

"You've been awfully kind to me, Eddie, considering

everything that has happened. And I shall always be grateful to you and your friends for rescuing me. I'm certain that I wouldn't even be alive right now if it wasn't for your efforts," Fiona said, her head turned away from him. "But now, I'm so uncertain about the future. It's hard to make any right decision."

"I understand, Fiona, I really do," Eddie said quickly. "My brother and I wandered since we were very young. It wasn't until last year when we were offered this ranch-hand job that we finally had a place to call home. Stability isn't something I've ever had 'til now. I know what it feels like to feel lost and unsure of what to do about it. So, take as long as you need to make that decision for yourself."

Eddie then took Fiona's hand and kissed the back of it before releasing it again. "I hope you sleep well, Fiona. I'm sure we'll see each other tomorrow. I look forward to hearing what you think of town," Eddie said as he stepped off the front porch stairs and started to make his way to the bunkhouse. If he didn't leave right away, then Fiona would certainly see his own tears at the thought of having to say goodbye to her if she did decide to return to Boston after all.

FIONA WATCHED as Eddie walked off the porch and headed towards the white bunkhouse. She stood watching him, her arms wrapped around her body as she thought about how it felt to have his lips on her hand. It was a very gentlemanly gesture that Fiona appreciated, and there was something about that kiss that sent warmth radiating throughout her body.

Fiona could only imagine what it would feel like to have his lips on hers. But before Fiona's thoughts could get the best of her, she turned away quickly and went back into the ranch house.

As Fiona made her way towards the hallway, she spotted Dr. Slater in the sitting room as he rocked his daughter to sleep. He was humming softly as he rubbed her back, her little eyes fluttering closed. Fiona couldn't help but smile as she looked at the picture of the two together. She also couldn't help but think what type of father Eddie would be. With the kindness he'd shown her, she could easily imagine Eddie being much like Dr. Slater in his affection and concern towards his own child.

After nodding to Dr. Slater and receiving a similar gesture in return, Fiona made her way down the hallway to the spare bedroom. She was looking forward to sleeping in a real bed. After closing the door behind her, she made haste in getting ready for bed, crawling under the thick comforter. It felt amazing to be able to lay her head down on a real pillow and feel the blankets around her. The bed was exceptionally comfortable, and Fiona knew that it wouldn't take long to fall asleep.

Ever since Bright Star had performed the cleansing ceremony, Fiona had finally been able to sleep through the night without being woken by nightmares. She would be forever thankful to Bright Star and the other men who had come to her rescue. As she lay in bed, she tried to think of a way she could personally thank them, or do something in return for what they'd done for her. They'd left their homes, families, and responsibilities behind in order to come to her rescue. No matter what she decided to do for herself, Fiona was determined to pay back their immense kindness.

As Fiona thought about her future, she tried to think about what her best option would be. Returning to Boston seemed like the sane thing to do. She missed the familiarity and safety she knew her home in Boston provided. She'd never experienced any sort of crime before, though she knew it existed in Boston. She was certainly missing the ease of her life back in that large city. Fiona tried to think if her life in Boston had really been worth running away from.

It took thinking of Eddie and comparing him to Mr. Crane for Fiona to start to remember what it had been like back in Boston. Though being kidnapped and almost dying had been very traumatic, her mind started to return to what she'd been facing whilst living with her parents. She started to remember the feeling of shame and despair after learning what her parents had planned for her. She knew that if it hadn't been for Mrs. Dickens, she'd have been married to Mr. Crane by now and forced to live underneath his roof.

Fiona pushed those fearful thoughts aside as she tried to think about her current situation. She was penniless and only had a few belongings that she could call her own. Her purse had been stolen and as far as she knew, nothing had been recovered from the robbers. She'd lost everything precious to her, to include the gold ring Mrs. Dickens had given her. Fiona knew that if she was going to stay in Spruce Valley, she would need to find some sort of employment. But what could she possibly do? She'd never worked a day in her life for payment, and knew only how to garden, do a bit of cooking, and mend simple clothing.

As Fiona closed her eyes, she willed herself to sleep. There was no point in worrying about her future right now. For tonight, she could simply sleep, and in the morning she would be able to see for herself all that Spruce Valley could actually offer her.

CHAPTER 14

By the time morning had come, Fiona was feeling more well rested than she had in years. She was quick to dress and get ready for the day. She didn't want to hold anyone up since she knew that Lucy and Martha would be traveling to town early that morning. After dressing in a simple gown Fiona could feel proud of, and having brushed and braided her hair, Fiona made quick work of her personal business before joining the Slaters.

"Good morning, Fiona. Yer looking well," Lucy said as she greeted Fiona in the kitchen. She was balancing Francene on her hip as she flipped flapjacks in the frying pan.

"Morning, Lucy. Here, let me take over on the stove since you have the little one," Fiona offered, as she took the wooden flipper from Lucy.

"Thank ye, me dear. Sometimes it can be a handful to cook for the crew and get ready to head into town for work," Lucy said with a sigh. "Women should be blessed with an extra set of hands when they give birth." Fiona laughed with Lucy at the very thought.

"Well, while I'm here, I want to earn my keep. You just let me know what you need help with, and I'll make sure to do it," Fiona reassured.

"I'll more than likely take ye up on that offer. I love managing the boutique in town and making all sorts of women's clothing, but I fear I'm lacking in my other duties here at the ranch," Lucy admitted as she bounced Francene around the kitchen, the little one becoming fussy. Fiona made quick work of finishing the flapjacks and brought them to the table for Lucy so she could feed her daughter. Fiona returned to the kitchen and began to fry the rest of the batter as the others soon joined them for breakfast.

By the time everyone had come to sit at the table,, Fiona had managed to not only finish cooking the flapjacks, but had sausage and bacon cooked and ready for serving. Fiona found it interesting that all of Dr. Slater's employees shared three meals a day with his family. She was starting to see that he was not only a kind person, but also a kind and considerate employer.

"Thank ye, Fiona, for helping out this morning," Lucy said as Fiona settled into a chair next to her. Across the way were Eddie and Sawyer, and the other cattle hand that Fiona had met as Tom.

"It was no trouble at all. It feels good to be doing something productive again," Fiona admitted.

"Well, with Sam havin' to leave early this morning to get to town and see his patients, I certainly appreciate it," Lucy replied as she fed Francene small pieces of flapjack and sausage.

"Grant's already out in the pasture. I plan to bring him something to eat after this," Sawyer spoke up.

"There is plenty to be done, that's for sure," Tom spoke up. Fiona watched as he ate his breakfast as quickly as possible, making Fiona fear that he'd choke. Fiona took her time eating, having a hard time breaking the habit of eating small bites at a time.

"Well ladies, thank you again for a wonderful meal. I'll be seeing you after a bit," Eddie said as he also quickly finished eating and stood from the table with the other ranch hands. Fiona watched him go, and right before he stepped out of the house, he looked back at her and gave her a wink. Fiona couldn't help but smile as Eddie left the ranch house. She was able to watch him from the window as he scurried after the others towards the barn.

"I think he likes ye," Lucy spoke up as she slowly rose with Francene, who needed a good scrub from the messy way she had eaten her breakfast.

"I think Eddie is just trying to be kind," Fiona said as she tried to do her best to quickly finish eating now that the men had departed. Lucy chuckled as she carried Francene out of the room.

"I'd say the man's in love," Lucy called from the other room. Fiona was shocked by this comment and stopped eating to ponder her words. Fiona listened to the sound of running water and a fussy Francene. Fiona guessed that the young one wasn't pleased about being washed. As Fiona looked out the window and watched Eddie ride out of the barn on a horse after the other two, she wondered if the man could have developed feelings for her already. And if so, how did she feel about that?

Fiona pushed the thought from her mind as she finished eating, then gathered all the dishes to be washed. By the time she and Lucy had finished cleaning up after breakfast, Martha was coming through the front door with Samuel in her arms.

"You ladies ready to head into town?" she asked.

"Absolutely. I can't wait to see everything," Fiona said in an excited voice.

"Well, come on then. I have the wagon out front," Martha said. Fiona eagerly followed Martha out of the ranch house with Lucy and Francene right behind her. Lucy climbed into the back of the wagon with the kids where they sat upon several hay bales. It took a moment, but Fiona finally found her footing on the wheel of the wagon in order to pull herself up and onto the front driver's bench.

"Yer already acting like a true Western woman, Fiona. Ye can get into a wagon all by yerself," Lucy said as she held the two small children on her lap as Martha flicked the reins and spurred the two horses forward.

"I've had a bit of practice these last few days as I rode in the covered wagon with Eddie and Sawyer," Fiona explained.

"That must have been an adventure all on its own," Martha commented with a chuckle.

"I cannot deny that," Fiona said as she joined in with Martha's laughter. "I quickly had to get used to sleeping in the wagon, riding in the wagon, and sometimes entertain Jack when he seemed to get moody and bored."

"Me goodness, does that monkey get under me nerves!

Jack once tore down all me curtains in a fit," Lucy said in an exaggerated voice.

"Jack once got cranky and started banging all the pots and pans together in the back of the wagon. Sawyer had been resting and caused him such a fright that I thought I'd never stop laughing," Fiona recalled. They all laughed over the thought, causing both the toddlers to join in with their laughter. When their mirth subsided, Fiona added, "And I think Bright Star has become quite fond of Jack. He even offered to take Jack south with him."

"I think that is a mighty fine idea. I can only imagine how that monkey might get in the way of you and Eddie properly courting," Martha said. Her words caused Fiona to go stiff with fear. She hadn't told anyone else besides Eddie that she was seriously thinking about returning to Boston. She only felt disheartened because she hadn't heard anything from her parents.

Seeming to notice her silence, Martha said, "I know you just got here, Fiona, but don't feel pressured about making any decisions right away. Eddie isn't going anywhere."

"And yer more than welcome to stay with us 'til ye can get settled," Lucy added. Fiona was truly touched by their kindness that at first, she didn't know what to say. Then an idea came to mind.

"The only thing I know I need to get settled is some sort of employment. I'm afraid I lost all my money on the journey out here when the robbers took everything," Fiona explained. She didn't like to speak about anything related to what she had experienced, but it was the truth.

"Well, you're more than welcome to help us out at the

shop. Having one more eye on the children would be a great help," Martha said.

"And I could use all the help I can get at home with feeding so many mouths. Yer a good cook, Fiona," Lucy added to the conversation. Fiona couldn't help but smile proudly.

"Thank you, Lucy. That means a lot to me since I was raised to never have the need to cook my own meals. I find pride in being able to take care of myself," Fiona admitted.

"As you should, Fiona. There is nothing more enjoyable than being an independent woman," Martha said.

"And I know how to mend clothing as well," Fiona added, as she remembered the needlework she'd been taught by Mrs. Dickens.

"That's fantastic. We're always getting clothes in the shop to fix," Martha said enthusiastically.

The three girls chatted the whole way into town. Fiona soon discovered that it was a good hour's ride to town, but the scenery was absolutely beautiful. Pine and oak trees dotted the horizon as wildflowers bloomed along the main road. They passed several other ranches and houses that the ladies were eager to tell Fiona about. The weather wasn't too hot in the early morning hours, but with few clouds in the sky, she reckoned that it would become warm as the day went on.

As the wagon rounded a bend in the road, Fiona caught site of town. There was a single main street that was lined with several businesses and stores. Fiona saw the Honeywell Inn, and across from it was the Sheriff's office. At the end of the street on the left was Mr. Frost's mercantile, and the church on the right. Behind that, Fiona could spot livery stables.

"It's not much, but it has everything you might want," Martha said as she led the wagon down the road,. She then stopped the wagon in front of the women's boutique.

"I think it's a quaint place, indeed," Fiona said as she stepped down from the wagon and went around to help Lucy and the children dismount. Then, they made their way to the front of the shop were Martha unlocked the door and ushered everyone inside.

Fiona was pleasantly surprised by the feminine decor of the shop, as well as the quality of the dresses she started to examine on the rack.

"I can tell you're from Boston, Lucy," Fiona spoke up as she turned to the woman. They had started straightening up the shop and pulling out mirrors and chairs for customers to use while visiting.

"I tried to design the shop based on me memory of other boutiques in the big city," Lucy admitted.

"You've done a justifiable job of that. It reminds me much of what I'm used to in Boston," Fiona admitted.

"Lucy designs and makes all the clothing while I take care of the paperwork," Martha said, as she stepped behind a central counter and pulled out a ledger book to show Fiona all their current orders.

"It seems you two are very busy," Fiona exclaimed as she read several lines.

"We've started to receive business from neighboring towns because Lucy is such a good seamstress," Martha explained.

"But we could use someone to greet the customers, keep an eye on the children, and tackle all the mending work," Lucy said as she steered Francene from a mannequin with a long gown that the little one was trying to pull over.

"Well, since I'm here, put me to work," Fiona said eagerly.

As the day progressed, Fiona got to mending the clothes that had been brought in for such work. Fiona sat at a chair and small table with all the needle and thread she could need. She focused on the work, but also on the children as Lucy worked mostly in the back of the shop, making gowns for various women in the community and from neighboring towns. Fiona had never felt this proud before as she tackled the pile of clothes that needed patching up or fixed in some way. She had envisioned herself doing some sort of work when she left Boston, and she was glad to be able to use the skills Mrs. Dickens had taught her to help the other ladies.

When lunch time rolled around, Martha agreed to stay behind while Lucy and Fiona took the children to The Eatery. Fiona had been so focused on her work that the morning seemed to pass by so quickly. But as she prepared to walk down the road to the small café at the back of the mercantile, she bent down and collected Samuel into her arms from where he'd been playing with a wooden toy horse.

"Come along, young man. We need to get something in that belly of yours," Fiona said as she tickled his tummy. The small boy giggled happily, causing Fiona to smile in return.

"Motherhood becomes ye," Lucy said with a wink as she picked up Francene and then made her way to the front door. Fiona blushed at the thought of having children of her own. She hadn't considered it before but assumed that with marriage, soon came children.

"You two have fun," Martha called as they left the boutique and headed down the boardwalk towards the café.

As they walked, Fiona enjoyed looking into the windows of the other shops. There was a furniture store with several beautiful pieces displayed in the window, but as Fiona continued on, she realized that many of the store fronts were empty.

"It seems that this town has room for more," Fiona commented.

"Sometimes I worry about this town. Sam explained that it used to be bustling when the local mine was opened and producing. But when the mine ran dry, everyone either left or had to find different employment," Lucy explained. As they walked, Fiona spotted the medical clinic amongst all the empty buildings.

"I sure hope that things continue to get better. I'm sure the town has benefited from having a women's boutique," Fiona said, trying to stay positive.

"I can agree with that, Fiona. I can't wait to see what happens next," Lucy said as she led them into the mercantile. There, Fiona was able to meet Mr. Frost and his wife, a very chatty couple. Then, Fiona and Lucy dined with the children at The Eatery were Fiona was introduced to Nell, the waitress, and was able to have the finest cup of tea of her life.

"My goodness, that is lovely," Fiona exclaimed after she had tasted the tea that Nell had expertly poured.

"I told you it was good," Lucy said with a chuckle. As the meal progressed, a very important fact popped into Fiona's head.

"Lucy, I don't have any money to pay for my portion of

the meal," Fiona said in a soft voice, leaning towards the other woman.

"I have enough, dear. With ye helping out at the boutique, I can cover our lunch," Lucy reassured. It was relief to hear, since Fiona wasn't sure what she was going to do about covering her expenses unless Lucy started to pay her for her work. But with everything the Slaters were willing to do for her, she didn't dare ask for pay.

As the day continued, Fiona couldn't wait to return to the ranch and tell Eddie all about her first day working in town with the other ladies.

EDDIE WIPED the sweat from his brow as he looked at the setting sun. It had been a long day out in the pasture as he helped move cattle, repair fences, and made sure to survey the other pastures for their progress on degrowing grass for the herd to be moved. As the summer faded to fall, it would be time to drive the best of the herd to market west, in Idaho. Just the thought of being on the road again after returning to Spruce Valley didn't settle well with Eddie. He wanted to spend every moment he could with Fiona while he still had the chance. That is why he had something special planned for them tomorrow, if he could get permission from the boss.

"Gray!" Eddie called as he rode in from the back pasture and made his way towards his boss.

"Yeah, Eddie?" Gray replied as Eddie came riding over to him. Gray had been keeping a close eye on the herd after hearing reports of wolves in the area.

"Do you care if I'm absent around lunch time tomorrow? I want to take Fiona out for a picnic," Eddie said, trying to keep confidence in his voice.

Gray smiled at him as he turned his eyes to Eddie. "So, you're going to try to take Fiona out on a date, are you?" Gray asked.

"Yes, sir, I am. I think it would be nice," Eddie said with an assertive voice.

"Well, make sure you let Mrs. Slater know. She makes the best picnic baskets," Gray said, turning his eyes back to the herd.

Eddie smiled as he said, "I'll make sure to do that, Gray. Thanks." Then he steered his horse and made quick work of getting back to the barn so he could put his horse away and get ready for dinner. After changing out of his work clothes and washing quickly with a wet cloth, Eddie changed into some clean clothes before taking Jack to his room.

"Now behave yourself, Jack. If you're good, I'll bring you something special to eat," Eddie said, as he handed the monkey two dates. The monkey jumped up and down on his bed as he screeched happily about having been given two dates at once. Eddie couldn't help but laugh at the monkey before he left the room, closing the door firmly behind him. Then, he walked quickly from the bunkhouse to the ranch house.

"Howdy, folks," Eddie called into the house as he entered. He made his way to the dining room to see that he was the first of the ranch hands to arrive.

"Hey there, Eddie. How did the day go?" Dr. Slater asked as he came into the dining room with Francene in his arms.

"Busy. There was plenty of work to get caught up on," Eddie said.

"I understand completely. I feel like every patient of mine came in today for their check up," Dr. Slater said with a sigh. "I'm not complaining about the good business, but I'm exhausted."

Eddie and Dr. Slater chatted for a while about ranch work as Sawyer and the rest of the ranch hands filed into the ranch house. By then, the ladies had started to bring dinner out to the table.

"Let me see that fellow," Gray said to Martha as he came into the house, reaching for Samuel. The little boy squealed with delight as he went to his father. As Eddie watched the interaction, he couldn't deny that he wanted that connection with a son or daughter one day. With that line of thinking, he looked towards Fiona as she sat across from him at the table. Their eyes locked until Dr. Slater spoke up and addressed Fiona.

"So, Miss Wilkins, what do you think of our small town here in Spruce Valley?" Dr. Slater asked.

Fiona's eyes moved from Eddie's as she smiled at the doctor. "I had a lovely time in town today. I think the women's boutique is marvelous, and there are several quaint shops in town," Fiona said with enthusiasm.

"Do you think that Spruce Valley is suitable for a woman from the East? Sheriff Ryder and I are always discussing ways that the town could be improved to hopefully attract more women to come here. There are plenty of men, but very few eligible young ladies," Dr. Slater explained.

"Honestly, I think it depends on the young lady. I myself

have never needed to do the things I must do now, in order to live comfortably. But I don't mind cooking, cleaning, and mending my own clothes. I find satisfaction in making something with my hands that others can enjoy," Fiona replied. Her words filled Eddie with so much pride, he felt that he might burst.

"It's hard for me to imagine a woman not being raised to know how to do those things," Tom spoke up before he took another bite of food.

"Oh, don't mind him, Fiona," Lucy said, making a shooing motion towards Tom. "He doesn't understand what it's like to live in a city." Fiona laughed then, the sound of her laughter a delight to Eddie.

"I agree that I could not imagine my acquaintances coming to live in a place like Spruce Valley. I think if you are born into wealth, then you become quite used to it and will more than likely seek it out in the future," Fiona said.

"But not ladies like us," Lucy added quickly. "We were born to pave our own way."

Dr. Slater then raised his cup in an effort to propose a toast. "To city women making a living in the West."

"Hear, hear!" Eddie called with the others as they toasted together.

"I surely would have it no other way," Lucy said, as she looked lovingly at her husband. Eddie watched them, thinking he wanted to experience that type of love with someone one day. And as he looked across the table, he caught Fiona's beautiful blue eyes once more and yearned to be able to have a real chance with her.

As the dinner progressed, the ladies happily chatted about

their day in town. It seemed to Eddie that Fiona was really starting to fit in and had been a huge help at the shop today. He only hoped that good days like today would convince Fiona to stay in Spruce Valley.

When the dinner was over, Eddie volunteered to help clean up. He wanted to find a moment to be alone with Fiona so he could ask her to accompany him on a picnic for lunch. Eddie carried dishes into the kitchen and started to scrub them, then Fiona dried them.

"I was wondering, Fiona, if you had plans for tomorrow?" Eddie asked as he cleaned a plate and handed it to her.

Fiona seemed to think about his question for a moment before saying, "I only thought that I would accompany the women to town again tomorrow to work at the boutique. I thought about posting a letter to Mrs. Dickens as well."

Eddie nodded as he remembered the housekeeper that helped Fiona escape Boston. "I was wondering if you might consider coming with me instead for a picnic," Eddie offered.

"Oh! I'll pack ye two a wonderful basket," Mrs. Slater said as she came into the kitchen, having heard what Eddie had asked. Eddie watched as Fiona blushed as she quickly dried the next dish and put it away.

"You don't mind, do you?" Fiona asked with concern in her voice.

"Not at all," Mrs. Slater assured. "Martha and I can look after things for a day."

"Well, if it's alright with you, I'd be happy to go on a picnic," Fiona said happily. Eddie felt relieved to hear Fiona's response. He was honestly looking forward to it. He quickly finished washing the dishes and helped to put them away.

"I'll be back in the afternoon to help you saddle up, and we'll go out to an empty pasture for lunch," Eddie said, smiling at Fiona.

"You mean I'm going to have to ride a horse?" Fiona asked, clearly surprised.

"You'll have to learn how to ride sooner or later. I'd be happy to teach you," Eddie said with a chuckle.

"I look forward to it," Fiona replied, squaring up her shoulders. The look of determination on her face made Eddie want to kiss her soundly on the mouth. But instead, Eddie bid her goodnight and made his way back to the bunkhouse. For the first time in his life, Eddie was looking forward to a picnic with a beautiful lady.

CHAPTER 15

iona was filled with excitement as she arose the next morning. She'd often daydreamed of riding a horse, much like the heroines in her novels. And the idea of getting to learn today from a handsome man was a thrilling thought of its own.

After Fiona dressed in one of her nicer traveling gowns, she made her way into the kitchen to help with the morning meal. She found Lucy and Dr. Slater talking in the kitchen in hushed words, and hating to disrupt a private conversation, she loudly cleared her throat as she came into the room.

"Oh, good morning, Fiona. How did ye sleep?" Lucy asked, quickly breaking her conversation the doctor as she looked towards Fiona.

"Very well, thank you," Fiona said. As she looked to Dr. Slater, she could tell that he was concerned about something. "Is everything alright?"

"Fiona, Sheriff Ryder stopped by …" Dr. Slater started to say when Lucy butted in.

"And wanted to see how ye were doing. We reassured him that ye are settling in here at the ranch just fine," Lucy said with a smile. She then went over to the stove where what looked to be eggs and bacon were cooking.

"Well, that's awfully nice of Sheriff Ryder to be checking up on me," Fiona said as she joined Lucy in the kitchen. Fiona jumped right in to helping Lucy prepare the first meal of the day but couldn't help but wonder what Dr. Slater had been about to say. It was obvious to Fiona that Lucy didn't want her to know right now, and she was fine with that. She was so excited about riding a horse today that she didn't want anything to ruin her first experience of it.

As Eddie and the others came into the ranch house, Fiona helped set the table. She smiled at Eddie, wishing it was already the afternoon. She couldn't wait to try her luck at riding a horse, and she couldn't deny that she liked the idea of Eddie showing her how to do it. All through breakfast, Fiona couldn't help but keep catching Eddie's eye, causing them both to smile at each other.

When breakfast was finished, Fiona volunteered to wash the dishes so Lucy and Francene could head into town with the kids. Lucy took a moment to pack Fiona a picnic basket that she could take with her later in the day.

"There's cheese and bread, and some apple pie I baked a few days ago. Surprised it was still in the ice chest," Lucy said as she set the picnic basket down on the counter for Fiona.

"Thank you so much, Lucy. I'm going to tidy up around

here and try my hand at doing laundry," Fiona said with a kind smile. Lucy chuckled at her enthusiasm.

"Just be careful with boiling the water for the wash all by yer own. I know yer familiar around a kitchen. I just want ye to be careful on yer own," Lucy said with concern in her voice.

"Don't worry, Lucy. I'll make sure to go slow. I'll take the wash outside and hang everything up to dry when I think I've finished," Fiona said, trying to reassure her new friend. The idea of having a true friend dawned on Fiona, and she thought she could never be happier.

"Well then, I shall see ye later," Lucy said as she picked up Francene and carried her out the door.

It had been a while since Fiona had been completely alone, and before her thoughts could run away with her, she quickly finished cleaning the dishes before gathering all the laundry.

Fiona quickly learned that washing one's own laundry was a timely process. But since she had very few clean garments and dresses, she was glad to have the opportunity to clean her clothes. After heating the water and dumping it in the washing pan, Fiona sat on a stool outside in the fresh air, and used the soap to wash her clothes thoroughly before hanging them up to dry.

By the time Fiona was done washing her clothes, she made her way back inside the house to see what else she could tidy up. But as she entered the kitchen, she found Eddie standing at the front of the house.

"Hey, there you are," Eddie said with a smile.

"Yes, I was out back washing my laundry," Fiona admitted with a smile.

"How'd that go?" Eddie asked with a smirk.

"I managed my own, thank you very much," Fiona replied as she tilted her head up.

Eddie chuckled as he shook his head at her in a playful way. "For a city girl, you could certainly pass for a Western woman," Eddie commented.

"Well, I'm certainly glad I could impress you," Fiona said in a flirtatious tone. She then picked up the picnic basket Lucy had prepared that morning. "Shall we be off?"

"Absolutely. I have a pleasant mare saddled and ready for you," Eddie said as he moved towards her and took the picnic basket from her hands. For a moment their hands brushed up against one another and Lucy couldn't help but imagine what it might feel like to be wrapped up in his strong arms once more.

Fiona focused her mind as she followed Eddie out of the ranch house. Tied to the front hitching post were two horses. Fiona recognized Eddie's gelding from yesterday and then turned her eyes to the chestnut mare that stood on the other side of him.

"This is Missy," Eddie explained as he led Fiona over to the mare. "She's a softy and should be suitable for your first horse."

"She's beautiful," Fiona said as she came to the side of the mare. She let her fingers graze across the horse's neck.

"Well, let's get you up into that saddle," Eddie said as he set down the picnic basket and neared Fiona. "You'll want to put your foot into the stirrup and push down with all your weight to lift yourself up into the saddle. Unfortunately, there isn't a sidesaddle in the barn, but you'll find riding this way to be more comfortable in the long run."

"I trust you," Fiona said lightly. For a moment, Fiona and Eddie stood smiling at one another before Fiona lifted her foot and placed it into the stirrup.

"Now, reach up your hand here and grab the saddle horn, and the other on the back of the saddle. Don't be afraid to climb up there. Missy knows what's going on," Eddie encouraged.

Knowing that Fiona simply had to go for it, she placed all her weight into her foot and pushed with all her might in order to pull herself up into the saddle and swing her leg over the horse. As she did so, she felt Eddie's strong hands guiding her up into the saddle, causing her to blush deeply. She'd never been handled so by a man and found Eddie to be both strong and gentle.

"Well look at you, Miss City girl," Eddie said with a chuckle. Fiona smiled with happiness as she shifted her weight in the saddle whilst holding on to the saddle horn.

"It's like learning to sail a boat," Fiona admitted, as she slid her other foot into the stirrup and tried to find her balance upon the horse.

Eddie chuckled. He untied the reins from the hitching post and handed them to Fiona, then retrieved the picnic basket and got on his own horse. "You'll be riding like you were born doing so by the end of the day," Eddie said with confidence, as he turned his horse away from the house. Fiona stilled her nerves as she followed Eddie's lead and pulled on the reins to steer Missy away from the ranch house and towards the gelding. Missy seemed to know which way to go as she followed closely after the other horse at a steady trot.

"I can't believe I'm riding a horse," Fiona said as she caught up to Eddie. The two horses trotted easily beside each other as Eddie led them along the white fence that enclosed the cattle pasture.

"You look good doing it, too," Eddie said with a wink. Fiona couldn't help but laugh as she looked down at her legs to see that they were slightly exposed from her dress, being raised up to accommodate riding in a saddle.

"That's because I'm rather scandalous in this position," Fiona replied.

"No, you look good because you look fearless, Fiona. I'm certainly proud of everything you've been able to accomplish since leaving Boston," Eddie said with pure seriousness in his voice.

"I don't know about being fearless, Eddie," Fiona reasoned as she looked at the scenery that stretched far in front of them.

"You've overcome a lot, Fiona. And it takes a certain type of woman to recover from what you went through. Any man would be happy to call you his wife," Eddie said in the same serious tone. Fiona went silent for a moment at the mention of being a wife. She knew that, originally, she'd come to Spruce Valley with the intention of not only avoiding being married to an odious man back in Boston, but to also give a relationship with Eddie a try. As they traveled together at a leisurely pace, Fiona couldn't help but observe Eddie and think that he would be a wonderful husband.

After a while, Eddie encouraged Fiona to increase Missy's pace. Putting her fear of falling aside, Fiona followed Eddie's directions thoroughly, and soon Fiona could feel the wind rushing by her as the horses trotted at a fast pace over the open prairie. Never had Fiona ever felt so free as she felt riding the strong horse beneath her, galloping happily.

Eventually, Eddie slowed his horse and Fiona followed suit. Up ahead, Fiona could see a single large oak tree that seemed to have been there for years. Eddie led her over to that tree, and after he dismounted and tethered the horses to the tree, he helped Fiona ease her way down from the saddle. As Fiona felt Eddie's strong hands on her waist again, she couldn't deny that she did enjoy the feeling.

With her feet firmly planted on the ground once more, Fiona found a decent place to sit and together, they settled down under the oak tree and enjoyed the lunch that Lucy had prepared.

"I can't believe how peaceful it is here," Fiona said at one point. They had been looking out over the open fields as a light wind blew across the grasses and wildflowers.

"I can only imagine how different it all is from being in the city," Eddie commented.

"It's very different, but in a good way. Certainly, things are more difficult here, but not impossible. I think more people would move out West if they realized how beautiful it was here," Fiona admitted.

Fiona noticed that Eddie went silent then, and she turned to look at him only to discover that he'd been watching her. She didn't know what to say and sat there looking at him, thinking him the most handsome man she'd ever met.

"Fiona, are you still thinking about returning to Boston?" Eddie asked. As soon as he said the words, guilt crashed over

Fiona. She was starting to feel foolish for ever having said such a thing.

"I don't think it is realistic that I'll go back. I haven't heard from my parents and I don't have the funds to make the trip back," Fiona explained. "But even if I did, after coming here and getting to know the area a little more, it reminded me of everything that I ran away from in Boston. I would be foolish to return there simply so I could live an easier life. That doesn't mean I'd be any happier."

As Fiona looked up at Eddie after she finished talking, she was surprised by how happy he looked. She couldn't help but smile at him in return.

"I can't tell you how happy it makes me to hear that you won't return to Boston. I was hoping beyond hope that you would decide to stay," Eddie said.

Fiona blushed again as she looked away from Eddie and instead on the wildflowers nearby. "It would be foolish to go back to Boston after realizing how wonderful it is here. Lucy and Martha have been the kindest ladies to me, and the fact that they were willing to offer me employment so quickly just goes to show what type of people they really are. I never had any real friends in Boston, but I believe I could here," Fiona said.

"Yeah, the Slaters continue to surprise me with their generosity. I truly enjoy working for them, but sometimes I dream of owning my own ranch, even if it's just a small herd of cattle," Eddie said.

"Really? What else do you dream about?" Fiona asked as she looked back at him, eager to know what his plans were for the future.

"Well, I'd like to own some land and build a decent house upon it. Eventually, I'd like a small herd of cattle that I could tend to and take to market each year. And I'd very much like to have a wife and a few kids, too," Eddie said as he looked at Fiona with much intensity. Fiona couldn't deny the pointed way in which he talked to her, and she was starting to suspect that he had strong feelings for her.

"That is an amazing dream, Eddie. I hope you're able to achieve it one day," Fiona said. As they finished their picnic and began to make their way back to the ranch house, Fiona wondered what her dreams were. What did she hope to obtain one day? But as she and Eddie returned to the ranch house after having a very pleasant picnic together, Fiona almost fainted from the sight of the two people standing on the front porch of the ranch house.

As EDDIE RETURNED to the ranch house with Fiona, he noticed two older people standing on the front porch. At first, Eddie assumed that they were patients of Dr. Slaters' who had come to his home in the hopes of catching him at home. But the closer they got to the ranch house, the more Eddie could see the fancy clothes they were wearing. And as Eddie looked to Fiona, he noticed how pale she'd become as she noticed them, too. It didn't take long for Eddie to realize who these two must be.

When Eddie stopped his horse in front of the porch, the couple turned to see them, their mouths falling open as Eddie dismounted, then helped Fiona down from her horse. She quickly straightened her dress and tried to smooth it.

"It's going to be okay, Fiona. I promise," Eddie whispered, taking her hand in his, giving it a gentle squeeze before leading her onto the porch.

"Never in my life would I expect my daughter ..." rose the voice of the older woman that Fiona resembled, to some degree. Her words were cut short as the man beside her raised his hand, silencing her instantly.

"Fiona, dear. We're glad to see you well," said the man. Eddie felt Fiona's grip tighten on his arm and he patted it to reassure her.

"Father, Mother. May I introduce you to Eddie Murtaugh. It's thanks to him and his friends that I'm alive right now," Fiona said in a voice that Eddie found rather odd. It lacked the warmth that Eddie was used to.

"Mr. Murtaugh, my many thanks for saving my daughter," said the man as he extended his hand toward Eddie. Eddie was quick to shake his hand, not wanting to be rude.

"It was my pleasure, Mr. Wilkins. The moment the news reached me, my friends and I set off to North Dakota to rescue Fiona," Eddie said, hating to bring up the fact that Fiona had ever been in such grave danger.

"Well, we'll be pleased to bring her home safely with us. We'll be leaving for the train depot in the morning," Mr. Wilkins said in a happy tone. But his words sent a shiver of fear running through him. And before Fiona could say anything, Eddie was quick to speak.

"Mr. Wilkins, I'd like to ask your permission for Fiona's hand in marriage. She is a wonderful woman that I'd be proud to call my wife. She enjoys being here in Spruce Valley, and I desire to bring her happiness for as long as I shall live," Eddie said, mustering every ounce of courage he could. His words clearly shocked Fiona's parents, as they did Fiona herself.

"There is no way ..." Mrs. Wilkins started to say, but Mr. Wilkins quickly silenced her once more. Eddie watched as Mr. Wilkins looked from him to Fiona.

"Fiona, my dear. Do you also wish to marry Mr. Murtaugh?" Mr. Wilkins asked. Eddie looked at Fiona then and watched as her eyes searched his. Then, as a smile crept onto her face, Eddie knew what her answer would be.

"Yes, Father. I'd be happy to have someone like Eddie for a husband. He's kind, hardworking, and very devoted to his boss. Eddie's the type of man I know I can trust to the fullest, and who will always encourage me instead of telling me what to do," Fiona said with a fierceness that Eddie had come to admire.

Eddie turned his eyes back to Mr. Wilkins as he waited to hear what the man would say. It was clear to him that Mrs. Wilkins wasn't pleased with what has happening, but Mr. Wilkins appeared to have the upper hand over his wife.

"After you ran away, Fiona, I was so terribly angry at what you'd done. We received such outlandish comments from our acquaintances that I was certain you'd planned to hurt us so. But when the news came that you'd been kidnapped, it didn't matter what anyone said. We came as soon as we could, but by the time we reached North Dakota, you were already gone," Mr. Wilkins explained. "And to see you well off, even riding a horse, it makes me think that perhaps you are better off here, with a man that can honestly protect you."

"I'll never let Fiona come to any harm," Eddie said reassuringly.

"And I'm certain of that," Mr. Wilkins replied. "And therefore, I'd gladly give you my blessing to marry Fiona, as long as she'll be happy the rest of her life."

Eddie couldn't help but smile as he hugged Fiona's arm to him. They looked at each other then, a deep feeling passing between them. Then, Eddie reached into his pocket and pulled out the ring he'd been carrying around ever since he found it. When Fiona saw it, her eyes went wide.

"Where did you find it?" Fiona asked as Eddie slipped the gold band onto her ring finger.

"When we rescued you, I found it and thought it meant something to you," Eddie explained. Fiona rubbed her finger over the gold band, thinking this was a complete miracle.

EPILOGUE

*W*ith her parents wanting to leave for Boston as soon as possible, Fiona and Eddie didn't have much time to prepare for their wedding. But with the help of all their friends, they were able to bring everything together in just two days.

Fiona never imagined when she ran away from Boston that one day, she would be walked down the aisle by her father on her wedding day. But low and behold, here she was now at the open doors of the church with her arm resting on her father's. Having borrowed Martha's wedding dress, Fiona was prepared for her big day. She could hardly believe that she was getting married, but she couldn't be happier.

"Once I return to Boston, I'll have your dowry money sent to you right away," Mr. Wilkins said softly to his daughter.

"Thank you, Father. You have no idea how much this means to me," Fiona said, as she looked at the man she'd loathed for most of her life.

"It's the least I could do after everything that's happened," Mr. Wilkins replied as the *Wedding March* began playing on the organ. At the sound of the music, Mr. Wilkins led his daughter down the aisle towards her waiting groom.

Fiona's eyes locked on Eddie as she came down the aisle towards him. He was handsomely dressed in a Western suit jacket and tie. They were also borrowed items, but Fiona reasoned that Eddie would look handsome in anything that he wore.

The church was filled with all their friends, and many people that Fiona was certain she would soon get to know as she started her life with Eddie. Even Bright Star had come to attend the wedding with his sons. As he sat next to Dr. Slater, he held onto Jack. Eddie had agreed to allow his beloved pet to travel with Bright Star so the monkey would have a more comfortable winter.

As Fiona reached the alter and came to stand in front of Eddie, her father sat down at the front of the church with her mother. Fiona held onto Eddie's hands as her body was overcome with such happy feelings. Reverend Paul began the ceremony as Fiona leaned close to Eddie.

"I love you," she whispered to him, causing him to smile brightly.

"And I love you," Eddie whispered back. They smiled at each other the whole way through the ceremony, and once they were pronounced husband and wife, Fiona experience a first kiss unlike anything she could have ever imagined. In that one kiss, she felt every ounce of love that Eddie had for her, as well as a promise of what their future together would be.

For the first time in her life, Fiona felt complete. She had found happiness with Eddie Murtaugh, and a home in Spruce Valley.

The End

Thank you for reading and supporting my book and I hope you enjoyed it.

Please will you do me a favor and leave me a review It would be very much appreciated, thank you

The Sheriff's Stubborn Secretive Bride (Book 4) Excerpt

To LEARN MORE CLICK/TAP on a link below.

Kindle USA

Kindle UK

KINDLE CA

Kindle AUS

WOMEN MUST EARN their own keep in this small Western town. But his choice for a wife has grand expectations...

Sheriff Josh Ryder longs for someone to come home to

every night. But the lawman's recent notoriety attracts so many replies to his mail-order bride ad that he has no idea if it's him or his name they're after. But he can't tear his eyes away from the photo of a stunning Georgia beauty.

Debutante Emily Middleton's dreams lie in the rubble of her father's bankruptcy. Now penniless, the young Atlanta socialite turns her attention to the West, hoping to secure a man who can live up to her standards. And when she flees her family to meet the rugged Montana lawdog, she's certain her ambition will soon be back on track.

Though the sheriff's immediately drawn to the feisty woman, he balks at her demands for a lifestyle beyond his means. And as Emily finds the handsome Josh simultaneously obstinate and dashing, she worries her fresh start could shortly turn sour.

Can the fiery couple fan their sparks into a sizzling sprint to the altar?

Excerpt:

CAST OF CHARACTERS

- **Eddie** & Sawyer Murtaugh, brothers
- **Fiona Wilkins**
- Dr. Sam Salter & Lucy Slater
- Gray & Martha Walters
- Sheriff Josh Ryder
- Bill Eckert, owner of the Honeywell Inn
- Greta Royal, widow and housekeeper
- Mayor Delphina Stavros
- Elena, Delphina's daughter
- Reverend Paul & Annette Gibbons
- Drake, Sheep farmer for Dr. Sam Slater
- Robert, Drake's brother
- Nell, waitress at the Eatery
- Zachariah Welliver, furniture maker
- Jensen Davis, ranch hand
- Tom Barker, ranch hand

AMELIA'S OTHER BOOKS

Montana Westward Brides series
#0 The Rancher's Fiery Bride
#1 The Reckless Doctor's Bride
#2 The Rancher's Unexpected Pregnant Bride
#3 The Lonesome Cowboy's Abducted Bride
#4 The Sheriff's Stubborn Secretive Bride

CONNECT WITH AMELIA

Visit my website at **www.ameliarose.info** to view my other books and to sign up to my mailing list so that you are notified about my new releases and special offers.

ABOUT AMELIA ROSE

Amelia is a shameless romance addict with no intentions of ever kicking the habit. Growing up she dreamed of entertaining people and taking them on fantastical journeys with her acting abilities, until she came to the realization as a college sophomore that she had none to speak of. Another ten years would pass before she discovered a different means to accomplishing the same dream: writing stories of love and passion for addicts just like herself. Amelia has always loved romance stories and she tries to tie all the elements she likes about them into her writing.

Made in the USA
Coppell, TX
21 May 2022